SPY HIGH:
MISSION ONE

SPY HIGH:
MISSION ONE

A. J. BUTCHER

LITTLE, BROWN AND COMPANY

New York ⋅ Boston

Little, Brown and Company

Time Warner Book Group
1271 Avenue of the Americas, New York, NY 10020
Visit our Web site at www.lb-teens.com

First U.S. Edition 2004

First published in Great Britain by Atom in 2003
Cover art by Jason Reed

Library of Congress Cataloging-in-Publication Data
Butcher, A. J.
Spy high : mission one / A. J. Butcher. — 1st ed.
p.   cm. — (Spy high ; #1)
Summary: As students at a special high school that trains them to be secret agents,
six teenagers struggle to complete the training exercises as a team before being
sent out into the field to sink or swim.
ISBN 0-316-73759-3 — ISBN 0-316-73760-7 (pbk.)
[1. Spies — Fiction.   2. Interpersonal relations — Fiction.   3. High schools — Fiction.
4. Schools — Fiction.   5. Adventure and adventurers — Fiction.]   I. Title.
PZ7.B9684Fr 2004
[Fic] — dc21   2003047604

10 9 8 7 6 5 4 3 2 1

Q-FF

Printed in the United States of America

PART ONE

Ben and Lori stood on the cliff top. Hundreds of meters below them they could hear the restless crash of the midnight surf against the rocks, but in the absence of the moon they could see nothing. Only the silver of their suits gleamed dully and seemed to shiver as they prepared themselves. To anyone who didn't know them, they could have been brother and sister, both tall, athletic, her blonde hair long, his cropped short. But they weren't brother and sister. Far from it.

"How much time do we have?"

"About an hour."

"Plenty, if the others manage to keep up." Ben turned his back to the cliff's edge and the sheer drop beyond. "Follow my lead."

He threw himself off the cliff.

Lori sighed. That was so Ben. He always had to go first, and without even a kiss. She'd remember that the next time he came looking for a little bit of lip action. But first things first. Repressing an urge to *whoop* her excitement while she did it, Lori too flung herself into thin air.

For the flimsiest of moments, as she gained the highest point in her leap, Lori seemed to hover far above the swirling ocean, as if gravity itself were pausing, considering whether to exert its weight on her or not. She thought of the coyote character in the old Road Runner cartoons — how many times he was left suspended and gasping in mid-air before plummeting to the bottom of a canyon. Still, as gravity decided not to make an exception for Lori Angel, and she started her plunging acceleration toward certain death, she had one rather important advantage over the coyote.

Lori swung on the rope clipped tightly to her belt, arced toward the black slab of the cliff, and relaxed her muscles as she'd been taught. The impact barely winded her. Her feet and fingers fixed themselves to the rock. No problem. If only the coyote had trained at Spy High, his whole career might have been very different.

A light winked at her from farther down the cliffside like a boy giving her the eye. That would be Ben. No doubt he'd already found the entrance to the tunnel and claimed it for the greater glory of himself. Lori rappelled toward him.

"Took your time," Ben commented. He'd already unclipped his line and was crouched in the narrow tunnel like a sprinter eager for the gun.

"I was admiring the view."

"Yeah, well, point your baby blues this way." Ben jabbed his finger toward deep, circular darkness. "A hundred meters to Stromfeld's complex. Let's put them behind us."

"So keen to save the world," Lori observed, with more than a hint of sarcasm.

"That's right," muttered Ben, "and if we reach the core before Daly, so much the better."

"Talk about the short straw," grumbled Jennifer Chen as she scrambled deeper beneath the earth, the roughly hewn tunnel showing no sign of coming to an end. "Ben and Lori get to rappel, Cally and Eddie get the sea approach, and what do we get?

The chance to crawl on our bellies all the way to the complex." She paused briefly to sweep the hair from her eyes. "How come we always get the short straw?"

Jake Daly, keeping close behind Jennifer, said nothing, though the expression beneath his tangled mop of black hair suggested that he had a good idea. He forced Stanton's smug face from his mind. *Concentrate on the mission,* he reminded himself. *Only the mission matters.*

"I just hope some of Stromfeld's goons get in my way," Jennifer warned darkly. "I've got a lot of tension I need to work off."

Jake frowned. "Forget it. We need to access the core as quickly and quietly as possible. We don't want any diversions."

"Says you. Me, I say what's a mission without the chance to break some faces? Hey, Jake . . ." Jennifer stopped, rapping her fist on the surface in front of her. The sound rang metallically. "We're in."

"We're in." Jake allowed himself a grim kind of grin, nothing too elaborate or emotional. They'd reached the fringe of Stromfeld's headquarters, as the steel plating of the tunnel now testified, but there was a long way to go yet.

They slithered across the polished metal plates. The light improved as they neared the main body of the complex, allowing Jake a rather more explicit view of his partner's rear as she wriggled her way forward. Jake was relieved that Eddie was not in his position at this particular moment.

Jennifer paused again — this time because she couldn't go any further. A wire grille blocked the intruders' path. She coiled back on herself and hissed to Jake: "Where's this supposed to lead again?"

"An empty storeroom," he supplied, "according to the blue-prints."

"Then send the blueprints back," Jennifer whispered. "And make that a very occupied storeroom." She indicated with her thumb.

Jake peered through the grille. A guard, uniformed and hel-meted in black and, more worryingly, equipped with a large and probably well-serviced laser rifle, was settling himself down on a packing case. They hadn't planned for this.

One problem at a time, Jake reminded himself. *Take nothing for granted.*

"What's he doing?" Jennifer mouthed.

By way of answer, the guard eased off his helmet and felt in his pocket, drawing out a packet of cigarettes and a lighter.

"Unscheduled work break," chuckled Jake. "Naughty boy. Well, we've only got to wait, sit quietly, and —"

"You can forget that," scoffed Jennifer. "I'm out of here."

"Wait!"

Jennifer didn't. Her feet smashed into the grille, sent it spin-ning across the storeroom and slamming into the far wall. The guard choked on the first drag of his cigarette, struggled to stand, and groped for his gun. He wasn't quick enough. Jennifer dropped lithely from the vent, smiled at the gape of astonish-ment on the man's face, and then lashed out with her right leg, pivoting on her hip. The kick struck the guard squarely on the side of the head. With a faint groan, he clattered to the floor. He didn't get up.

"Somebody should have told you," Jennifer tutted. "Smok-ing's bad for your health."

*   *   *

They dragged the dinghy up onto the shingle and over to where the angle of a lurching rock would hide it, and then crouched in the shadow of the same rock to take stock.

Eddie Nelligan didn't look good, his naturally reddish complexion tinged with green. "Water," he said with a moan, "should be strictly reserved for washing with. That's not an ocean, it's nature's way of making you throw up. Why can't we have missions to nice, sunny, tropical islands in the middle of nice, calm, flat seas? What's the fascination with shaky tides and the middle of the night?"

"Eddie," prompted Cally Cross, "do the words 'let's,' 'keep,' and 'moving' mean anything to you?"

"I mean, it's not asking for much, is it? Look at the Bond movies. An island like Dr. No's wouldn't be too bad, would it? Great beach, bit of a waterfall, a few palm trees. There's got to be an island like that owned by a full-time nut somewhere in the real world, hasn't there? Why can't they send us there? And if they could throw in a Bond girl as well, that'd sure increase my motivation."

"'Fraid you'll just have to put up with me," said Cally. "And as for motivation, if you don't get moving now I'm going to be motivating you by squeezing somewhere that hurts."

"Cally," Eddie said, drooling, "do you know how long I've waited for you to say that?" But he got to his feet and followed his partner just the same.

They moved as smoothly and silently as they could across the craggy scrap of shore that spilled out of the cave. Cally glanced up at the cliff, wondering how the other pairs were faring in their joint mission. Returning her gaze to the mouth of the cave, much closer now, she wondered whether they, too, were finding further progress barred by Stromfeld's men. There were two of them, armed and looking as alert as could reasonably be expected of somebody on guard duty at midnight.

"We could try and creep past them," she suggested to Eddie.

"I don't do creeping," he returned. "It makes me feel like I've got something to hide. Besides, I bet these guys have been working really hard and could do with a bit of a rest. And I think we can help them with that."

"Sleepshot?"

"Sleepshot. You want the one on the right or the left?"

In unison, Eddie and Cally raised their right arms. Starlight glittered on shiny metal wristbands. They lowered their hands and pointed their wrists at their respective targets. With a hardly audible *phut*, tiny twin projectiles spat from their wristbands.

The countless hours of practice paid off. The sleepshot shells buried themselves in the guards' bare cheeks. They drilled into the skin, immediately releasing a powerful anaesthetic into the bloodstream. Neither man would wake before dawn.

"Nighty night," crooned Eddie. "Sleep tight. Don't let the bedbugs bite."

"Hey, Eddie," said Cally exasperatedly, "before you start breaking into bedtime stories, we've got work to do, remember?"

Eddie eyed the forbidding-looking cave and the cliff piled high above it. "How could I forget?" he said. "I hope Stromfeld's got an elevator."

"These corridors all look the same," groaned Lori in frustration. "Do you think Stromfeld bought them all in one big job lot at a corridor sale somewhere?"

"Don't you pay attention in Psychology, Lori?" Ben grunted.

"It's the mentality of the megalomaniac. Studies have shown that would-be rulers of the world are almost always deeply obsessive and can't tolerate change. That's why they want to impose their will on the rest of us. Keeping every area of his complex identical is Stromfeld's way of proving he's in control and can dictate even the appearance of the environment."

"That's another A-grade essay in the making there, Ben," Lori said. "But even if you're right, that's not much good to us. Unless Stromfeld's put up signposts, we still haven't got a clue which way to go to the core."

Lori had a point. She and Ben had penetrated Stromfeld's underground headquarters straightforwardly enough, using the tunnel from the cliffside leading to a little-used section of the complex, but since then they'd spent a good twenty minutes wandering an apparently inexhaustible supply of featureless metal corridors. And when you were working under a deadline — a serious deadline — that was not good. At least they hadn't encountered any of Stromfeld's goons yet, though Lori was beginning to hope that they might run into one soon, if only to ask directions.

Ben was frowning — he tended to take even the slightest note of criticism personally. Okay, so they hadn't quite made the progress he'd expected, but he'd put money on the others being farther behind. They had to be. "I thought I'd memorized the blueprints, but I guess there's no harm in activating the belt-brain."

He pressed a stud in his belt. A beam of light stabbed from the buckle and resolved itself into a holographic image of the floorplan of the complex. Three pairs of red dots flashed at various points on the plan.

"There's us," Lori pointed, as delighted as if she were meeting an old friend.

"Yeah, and there's the core," observed Ben, "the nerve center of Stromfeld's entire operation, and there are Jenny and Daly . . ."

"Closer to the core than we are," Lori thoughtfully completed Ben's sentence for him.

Not looking happy, Ben pressed his belt stud a second time. Now a flashing red line appeared on the plan, starting from the two circles that represented himself and Lori and leading, like somebody tackling a maze in a puzzle book, to the core. Their path was all mapped out for them. All they had to do was follow it.

"Ben?" Lori was already starting to move off. "Weren't we in a rush?"

Apparently not. Ben was motionless, scrutinizing the hologram, paying particular attention to the distance between Jake and Jennifer and the core on the one hand, and the distance between him and Lori and the core on the other. Assuming he and Lori obeyed the recommended route, Ben estimated there was no chance they could get to their destination before the other two. And that was *not* an acceptable outcome. If, however, he and Lori took a right up ahead, instead of a left, then they'd save time for sure — save time and get the jump on Daly. . . .

He strode forward purposefully.

"Er . . . Ben?" Lori tried again. "The belt says left."

"Yeah, well, I say right."

"Excuse me? These routes have been worked out by the logistics guys at Spy High —"

"— And none of them are here in Stromfeld's lair with us," Ben pointed out. "They don't know. They can't tell us what to do now." To emphasize the fact, he pressed his belt stud once more. The hologram collapsed meekly in on itself, leaking back into his buckle like water down a drain. "We're on our own and we'll save time if we go the way I say. We'll complete the mission more quickly."

"I don't know, Ben. They ran all kinds of tests to find the clearest route . . ." Lori's brow creased in doubt.

"It's called initiative, Lori," Ben urged. "Come on. Trust me, okay? I need you."

And she was persuaded. When Ben gazed at her like that — earnestly, piercingly, like he could see right into her heart — she couldn't resist him at all. When he looked at her that way she'd do anything. Even if he told her to go knock on Stromfeld's door and give herself up. And in that context, taking a right instead of a left didn't seem such a big deal after all.

Especially as the corridor into which the two of them turned bore some kind of identification: C-ALPHA. Apparently Ben *was* right.

"C for core?" she suggested, pleased by the renewed expression of eager determination on his face.

"C for closer, that's for sure." Ben paused by a door, whipped a deactivator from his belt, and placed it over the lock mechanism. "We're almost there."

But as the deactivator did its work, Lori found those annoying doubts returning. *Why* was *this area shaded on the plans?*

The door slid open.

Ben grinned and offered Lori his hand.

They stepped through.

At least a dozen laser rifles pointed directly at them.

"Welcome," said a voice. "How nice of you to drop by."

It wasn't often that intruders were so accommodating as to walk right into a guard room.

* * *

A series of dull thuds echoed down the corridor. Jake tensed. "You get the feeling something bad's just happened?" He sniffed the artificially regulated air as if the stench of something rotten had just wafted through. He grimaced. "I don't like it."

Jennifer sensed nothing amiss, but even though she'd only known Jake a short time, less than a term, she was already beginning to trust his instincts. There was something preternatural about him, something almost animal. She tensed her limbs for action, glanced behind. The corridor gaped innocently empty in both directions. "You think that guard might have recovered?"

"The way you hit him, I doubt he'll ever recover. And we tied him up pretty good." Jake's expression was dark, intense. "But something's wrong. I'm switching to radar vision."

"Agreed."

The partners yanked what seemed like thin strips of plastic film from their belts and wrapped them around their heads to cover their eyes. As the two ends connected at the back there was an activating click. The film joined and stiffened and instantly their fields of vision expanded. By shifting the focus of their eyes only slightly, Jake and Jennifer could now visualize any object, animate or inanimate, that was behind them, on either side of them, or even through adjacent walls. It was difficult to creep up on a student of Spy High.

"How is it for you, Jen?" Jake checked.

"Three hundred sixty degrees perfect. I'm seeing the circle."

They continued their passage through the endless corridors, moving like shadows. Everything was looking good, but Jake still couldn't shake the premonition that they were on the brink of disaster. Maybe the two figures ahead of them, certainly guards, out of human sight around a corner but clearly picked out by radar vision, had something to do with it. Jennifer squeezed his shoulder to indicate that she'd detected them too.

"Sleepshot," said Jake.

Jennifer shook her head. "Sorry. A girl needs her exercise."

She was running to the corner before Jake could stop her. He cursed softly under his breath. He had no doubt that Jennifer could deal with a pair of Stromfeld's men — in fact, he felt almost sorry for them, but physical combat simply wasn't necessary at this stage. He heard the dull thud of boot against chin, the meaty chop of hand on neck. It was like back in the storeroom. Jennifer took too many risks. One of these days it was going to cost her.

But maybe not today. Jake rounded the corner to find her posing over the bodies of the two poleaxed lackeys like a hunter with her spoils. "Jake," she grinned, "you missed all the fun."

Jake tore off his radar vision. "This is not supposed to be fun." His voice was cold. Jennifer bridled at the sound of it. "This is supposed to be a mission. We always use sleepshot where we can. Sleepshot's effects are guaranteed."

"What's all this *we*?" Jennifer retorted. "You don't own me, Jake. You can't tell me what to do. And let me tell *you* something —" she clenched her fists theatrically — "these are guaranteed too."

Behind her, a groan.

"Jen!"

One of the guards, not quite unconscious, was reaching inside his tunic. Jennifer stamped down on his neck, a mere fraction of a second too late.

All around them, stridently, deafeningly, like a net of sound thrown over them, came the blare of the alarm.

Eddie and Cally heard it as they arrowed their way in an elevator from the lowest levels of the complex to its very heart. Eddie cocked his ear: "Interesting choice of muzak."

"Means trouble, Eddie," Cally said unnecessarily. "We've got to be ready for anything."

"Don't worry." Eddie refused to appear concerned. "I carry protection with me at all times." The elevator's rise ended almost imperceptibly. Its doors slid open silently. "Looks like this is our floor."

They edged out into a trademark Stromfeld corridor cautiously, which was probably just as well. They were greeted by a barrage of laser blasts, sparking off the wall beside them, so close Cally felt her hair singe.

"Pleased to meet you, too," Eddie muttered.

A handful of goons charged toward them, firing wildly. *If they'd only stop to take proper aim, they'd be taking out more than just scenery*, Eddie mused, *but that was probably why these guys had never been promoted beyond the level of the hired help*. He and Cally didn't make the same mistake. Dropping to one knee in perfect unison they brought sleepshot into play, firing from their wristbands with unerring accuracy. Two attackers fell . . . four, six. But whether the others might then have retreated or not never became an issue: The scorch of a laser blast against Cally's boot alerted her to the sudden appearance of reinforcements from the other end of the corridor.

"Eddie!" she cried, firing off a sleepshot shell behind her. "Too hot for comfort!"

"Then let's cool off," Eddie agreed, darting back into the elevator.

Cally leapt after him as the doors slid shut. Laser blasts ricocheted off steel, but for the moment the two were safe. "Where now?" Cally gasped.

Eddie jabbed a button and the lift swept upward.

"There are just so many choices. Tenth floor: weapons of mass destruction. Twelfth floor: interrogation and brainwashing. Fifteenth floor: master plans for world domination. It's a great day out for the whole family at Stromfeld and Co." He punched the emergency button and the elevator obeyed, lurching to a stop between floors.

"And that helps us *how* exactly?" Cally demanded. "Do we just make polite conversation till they override the system?"

Eddie appraised his companion thoughtfully. "Surely we can make the time pass more pleasurably than that." He winked. "What about hopping up on my back for a start?"

"Eddie, I knew you were twisted, but —"

"Cally, please!" Eddie was the shocked innocent. "How else are we going to bust the hatch unless you climb on my back to reach it?"

"Huh?"

"If we climb up the cables, Stromfeld's boys won't have a clue where we are. It works in the movies every time."

"Is that right?" Cally said skeptically. "Well let's hope Stromfeld's on the same script."

They worked quickly. Cally used the laser cutter from her belt to blow out the hatch, then hauled herself out to balance on the roof. She gazed dubiously up at the yawning elevator shaft and the thick cable that she was expected to scale. Not for the first time, it occurred to her that life had been a lot easier on the street.

"What are you worried about?" Eddie jibed gently as she pulled him through. "Just imagine you're back in the gym at Spy High."

Cally forced herself to focus. "The only thing I'm worried about," she retorted, "is you coming up behind me."

They climbed steadily, wrapping their feet around the cable and pulling themselves up hand over hand. It was as well that they had no fear of heights, as soon the elevator was lost in the shaft's general gloom.

They passed the dim outlines of several doors before Cally paused and yelled down, "What about getting off here?"

"I can't think of any reason why not," Eddie called back.

The doors slid smoothly open and a dozen guards trained laser rifles on them.

"Or maybe I can." Eddie smiled sheepishly at the guards. "Elevator engineers. We hear you've been having a few problems. . . ."

"Let's look on the bright side," Eddie said. "We wanted to get to the core. That's where we are. I think Mr. Stromfeld deserves a vote of thanks for helping us out."

"Why don't you just shut up for once?" snapped Ben. He didn't share Eddie's optimism, and there was no logical reason why he should. All right, so the first aim of their mission had been to penetrate the nerve center of Stromfeld's operation, which technically they'd done, but the second and most important objective had been to sabotage Stromfeld's equipment before he could launch destructive strikes on major cities.

Achieving *that* was going to be extremely difficult. The six members of Bond Team had been stripped of equipment and surrounded by a gaggle of guards, outnumbering them at least three to one. Ben felt anger and frustration well up in him like a bitter poison. How could they possibly salvage the mission now? How would almost-certain failure reflect on his leadership of the team and on his future at Spy High? He found himself automatically glaring across at Jake Daly. At least that was one consolation, however minor: Daly was in an equally undistinguished position.

Jake noticed Ben's stare but ignored it, concentrating instead on absorbing the details of the core, specifically the three screens, each displaying the glittering, gleaming shell of a bomb, trembling and eager to go about its business. Computers were arranged around half the circumference of the room, where bespectacled technicians were tapping in launch procedures. The core was shaped like a funnel, tapering inward to a point above them from which hung a giant black metallic ball that flickered with peacefully green lights. Its purpose Jake could not guess. Maybe Stromfeld was into mood lighting. One thing was certain, his mood at the moment would be triumphant with a capital "T." Triumphant to the point of arrogance and beyond. And arrogant people made mistakes. Jake was happy to wait for Stromfeld to make his.

"Concentrate," he murmured to the group. "And watch for an opening." This wasn't over yet.

"Ah, my little group of interlopers."

The Big Entrance.

Stromfeld swaggered into the core, flanked by his grimmest, meanest-looking guards. "So sorry to have kept you waiting, but for the crowning moments of one's life, one has to look just right, yes?"

The man who smiled complacently at Bond Team was wobblingly fat, his thinning hair greased down on his forehead. He sported an impeccably manicured, Hitleresque moustache, no doubt to complement his equally pristine SS uniform. His boots gleamed like they'd spent the last three days being polished.

"Nazi retro," scoffed Eddie. "Is this guy passé or what?"

Stromfeld regarded Bond Team condescendingly, sighed in exaggerated disappointment, and shook his head. His corpulent jowls quivered. "Children," he observed. "They send children to distract me. Such foolishness merits their destruction, yes? How old are you all, hmm? Fourteen? Fifteen?"

"I'm actually thirty-five," piped up Eddie, "but I exercise every day. Maybe you should give it a try yourself."

"Very amusing . . . for a *little boy* in his last moments of life," said Stromfeld humorlessly. "Perhaps you are wondering why you are not already dead, yes?"

"Natural generosity?!" Jake ventured, looking worriedly at Jennifer. There was something caged in her eyes, desperate. They had to act soon or she was likely to get herself killed. If only Stromfeld would hurry things along.

Their captor chuckled ripely, as only a fat man can. "Not quite. Not quite."

"I know," sneered Ben. "As a paid-up member of Maniacs Anonymous you want a chance to boast about your master plan, to brag about how it's going to be when you're ruler of the world, master of all you survey and all that crap, and you need an audience. Pity it's got to be a captive audience."

"How very perceptive," admired Stromfeld. "Perhaps we'll execute you last, yes?"

"You're just a cliché, Stromfeld," groaned Ben. *Play on their vanity*, he remembered from spycraft lessons. *Puncture their sense of self-importance. Make them mad.* "You're just an entry in a textbook. A porker in a uniform."

Stromfeld waggled a finger as thick as a sausage in Ben's direction and laughed uneasily. "What I am, boy," he corrected, "is the future. For when my bombs have erased every last vestige of your decadent and degraded culture from the face of the earth I will build a new society from the ashes of destruction. A society governed only by me, shaped in my image forever."

"Bit overweight, then," said Eddie.

"And *that* is why you're still alive — to witness the first fiery beginnings of the Age of Stromfeld. Technicians!" Stromfeld drew himself up massively. "Let fly the bombs!"

"Ben!" cried Lori desperately.

The technicians' fingers sped across their consoles. On one, two, all three screens a missile launched, rising from their hidden silos and slicing the air like knives. In minutes they would reach their targets. In minutes the world would enter a new dark age. Unless Bond Team could stop them.

"Cally," hissed Jake, "what do you think?"

"I've seen enough," Cally calculated. "I can bring them down."

"Great, because I've had it with this guy."

"Wait for it, Daly," cautioned Ben.

"Hold them!" At Stromfeld's order, the guards gripped Bond Team's arms more tightly yet. "Wait for what? A miracle?"

"No, fat boy," growled Jake. "The mistake you've just made."

Ben's eyes narrowed. "Let's give these jokers the shock of their lives."

The crackle of electricity charged the air. The guards holding the teenagers yelped and recoiled as electric current surged from the material of Bond Team's suits and jolted through them. Some collapsed at once, others needed further encouragement from fists and feet.

"In case you're wondering," Eddie supplied, as he threw one man over his hip and elbowed another viciously in the jaw, "they're called shock suits. They're not available in the shops but if you send a very large check to Spy High, you never know your luck."

"Stop them! Stop them!" Stromfeld commanded. "Protect the computers!"

The remaining guards waded in, but in such an enclosed space, rifles were useless. They dropped like flies.

A sequence of blows from Jennifer and Jake ended the technicians' interest in the evening's proceedings, allowing Cally to seat herself at a console and work with breathtaking speed at the keyboard. This was what she was in the group for, she knew — her wizardry with all things technological. While the others had watched Stromfeld or weighed up the guards, her eyes had been totally devoted to these systems, to assimilating and memorizing what the technicians had done, to girding herself to break the codes and destroy the missiles before they could reach their destinations. She punched a final combination.

"Yes!" The bright casing of the first missile blistered and burst, a second sun in the sky. The screen died with it.

Two bombs left. Cally glanced feverishly at the counter. Two minutes of time.

Stromfeld raged as his dreams died around him. He glared at the girl, at the screen, and back at the girl. His puffy eyes narrowed.

"You!" he yelled to a dazed but conscious guard who still had hold of his rifle. "Shoot her!" At least one of his bombs would get through. It wouldn't be fair otherwise.

The guard took a shaky aim. Fired. And a scissor kick from Lori slammed into him.

Somebody screamed.

Somebody fell.

Stromfeld.

"What's going on?" cried Cally, not averting her gaze from the screens for a second.

"We'll deal with it," Jake said. "Just get rid of those bombs."

"Yes, *sir!*" She punched another code. A second dazzling scar in the sky. A second screen plunged into darkness. Cally clenched her fist in triumph.

Only one missile left now. And sixty seconds of time. Cally saw it arc, descend, accelerate. Far below it, but not *so* far below it: land, cities, people, oblivious to their imminent fate. Teeth gritted, Cally redoubled her efforts.

The few remaining guards threw their weapons down and their hands up. With Stromfeld gone, there was little point to their fighting on. Who would pay them? Lori and Eddie herded them together as Ben crossed to Stromfeld's body. He felt like shouting for joy. The mission was on the brink of success after all. How they'd applaud him back at Spy High! Cally was about to destroy the final missile and its creator was —

Alive.

Just.

And grinning, blood trickling from both corners of his mouth. He didn't seem to have a lot to grin about, given the gaping wound in his considerable belly, but maybe the control pad he held in his trembling hands had something to do with it, the pad on which he was punching in numbers. . . . Ben knocked it from his grasp, sent it skittering across the floor.

"Too . . . late . . . ," breathed Stromfeld. Above him, the black metallic ball began to descend. "Even as . . . you win . . . you lose." Its green lights, one by one, were turning red. "Another . . . bomb . . . too big to evade . . . *boy*. So down we go to Hell . . . together . . . yes?"

"Oh, my God." Ben didn't care whether Stromfeld's suddenly staring eyes and lolling head meant he was dead or not. He had a more pressing priority now. "Get over here! Everyone but Cally!"

"What is it?"

The ball paused some five feet off the floor. A number display was counting down from sixty. Inexorably. Inevitably. Unstoppably.

"It's a bomb. It's gonna blow. Cally can't help us."

"Wait!" Cally was crying out. "I'm nearly there. I'm nearly . . ."

She could see the city now, its buildings basking in the peaceful afternoon. She could see the victims.

"Do something, Ben!" urged Lori.

"Okay, okay. That class we had in bomb defusal . . ." He scrambled for a laser rifle and shot at the lower part of the metal casing.

Cally jumped. For a second, distracted. And with less than sixty seconds to play with, that was long enough. For the first and fatal time, her fingers faltered.

The faces of people she didn't know were gazing up from parks and pavements, the bomb upon them like the crack of doom. Herself screaming uselessly: "Too slow! Too slow!"

The screen showed impact. Mushroom clouds branded to Cally's eyes.

"This can't be happening!" Lori wailed. "It can't . . ."

The guts of the metal bomb were exposed, its intestines of wires and cables. The number display was at thirty-five, thirty-four . . .

"I know this type of device," Ben was claiming. "We studied it in class. It's really very simple, basic. These two wires —" the others saw them, delicate, deadly — "red. Blue. Red detonates the bomb at once. Blue defuses it. So all I need to do . . ." Ben's fingers fluttered.

"NO!" Jake seized Ben's hand in a grip of iron.

"What do you think you're doing?"

. . . twenty-one, twenty . . .

"You're wrong, Ben. It's the other way around."

Ben wrenched his hand away fiercely, shoved at Jake. "What do you think *you're* doing? I'm never wrong."

"Cally!" Lori pleaded. "Cally, get over here!"

But Cally was helpless, wild eyes staring blankly in front of her.

"Trust me, Ben, this time —"

"No!"

. . . ten, nine . . .

"Will one of you do something?" Jennifer shouted. "Jake . . ."

. . . five, four . . .

"No! Jake's not leader. I . . ."

. . . one . . .

"Would you believe it?" grunted Eddie.

. . . zero.

The world turned white.

And stayed white, as blank and empty as the mind of an amnesiac.

"So this is death," observed Eddie. He felt his shoulderblades, passed a hand above his head. "No wings. No halo, either. Guess we didn't make the grade as angels."

"Angels they can keep," scowled Ben. "It's making the grade at school that counts. And thanks to you, Daly, we've got problems." He advanced toward Jake across the void. There was an anger and a frustration in him that he was making little attempt to control. Jake stood with his arms crossed and his stare fixed, unintimidated, unimpressed. "I mean, where do you get off challenging my authority in the field like that? *I'm* team leader. Me. And that's supposed to mean something."

"It does." Jake frowned at the forefinger Ben was jabbing at him. "It means I haven't broken off that finger you've got in my face. But if you don't put it away, like now, I promise you you'll never look the same in gloves again."

"Is that a threat, Daly? Are you threatening me?"

"Ben, this is getting us nowhere," Lori stroked her hands over his shoulders. "You can't just blame Jake. We all messed up."

"That's right," Jennifer struck in. "There's six of us in Bond Team. It's not just about the two of you." She cupped her hands at Jake's ear. "Do you hear that, Mr. Macho Man?"

"Okay, okay. So we're all to blame."

But some, Ben thought darkly, *more than others.* He was glad that Daly didn't offer to shake hands.

"Excellent," approved Eddie, and look, now that we're all friends again, united in a sense of common failure, here comes Saint Peter. Hey, Saint Pete, did you send the Pearly Gates away for refurbishment? And what happened to the beard and the long white robes?"

"Nelligan, if you devoted half as much energy to your spycraft as you do to your inane chatter, you'd graduate within a week and Spy High could say goodbye to you forever. Sadly for us all, that doesn't appear likely, does it?"

The man who materialized in what had previously been innocent white space did not look like a saint, Peter or any of the others. Unless there was a saint of boxers, as grizzled and as battered as any fighter, who dressed in soldier's fatigues and spoke in a voice like boots on gravel. Corporal Randolph Keene regarded Bond Team with sharp, critical eyes, his head swiveling on its bull neck.

"Corporal, I know it looks bad. . . ." Ben was thinking damage limitation.

"We got to the core, though, didn't we, and we stopped two of the bombs." At least he could rely on Lori to loyally back him up.

"You failed," Keene snapped. "You did what no team at Spy High can afford to do. You failed your mission. Totally. Completely. Utterly. Absolutely. Abjectly. Pathetically. Disastrously. Unforgivably."

"So, Corporal," interrupted Eddie, "if you were giving marks out of ten . . ."

Keene pressed a stud on his I belt. "I'm ending the program. Stand by for transfer."

The white world trembled like cowardice. It flickered with sudden night.

The glass shields of the cyber-cradles hissed and rose, releasing the teenagers from the digital drama of the Stromfeld program into the rather less exotic environment of the school's virtual reality chamber. They sat up, blinking, rubbing their eyes. The transfer from one realm of experience to the other always took a little bit of adjustment.

But they were used to Corporal Keene standing there, waiting for them.

"Senior Tutor Grant's study." He glowered. "Thirty minutes." The silence that followed was heavy with *or else.* Keene turned smartly and stomped his way from the chamber.

"You can never see Keene playing Santa Claus, can you?" Eddie noted.

"I don't know." Lori hauled herself out of her cradle, shook her limbs and stretched. "Corporal Keene, he's always so bad-tempered, I never know whether he really means it or not."

"He means it now," Jake said. "There's never any joke about Stromfeld."

"Then are we really in trouble?" Jennifer paused in the arching of her back. "They can't fail us for this, can they? We get another chance, right? Ben?"

Ben glanced at Jake. It was a petty triumph that Jennifer had directed her question to him rather than to his rival, but maybe the only one of the day. He wasn't too proud to make the most of it. "Come on, Jen, you remember the rules. They told us at the start of term. Each team gets three attempts at the Stromfeld program. Three strikes and you're out. Non-negotiable. We're two down now."

"But that's . . ." Jennifer seemed to be struggling to comprehend the situation in a mixture of defiance and despair. "But that's just . . . we can't fail. *I* can't fail. You don't understand. I've got to graduate."

"Well," Ben said pointedly, "maybe some people ought to remember that the next time they feel like questioning a team leader's decisions in the field. I'm going for a shower."

As always, Lori followed after Ben, but this time Jennifer did too, still pressing for further information. Jake waited until they'd left, then thoughtfully slouched off himself.

Eddie watched Cally. She hadn't actually climbed out of her cyber-cradle yet. She was sitting up in it hunched forward, almost like she wanted to be sick. Maybe she did. It occurred to Eddie that she hadn't said a word since their virtual deaths in the Stromfeld program.

"You okay?" he asked cautiously. Intimate inquiries into somebody's health or otherwise were not one of Eddie's strong points.

"No."

"You want me to fetch a bucket or something?"

"Is that supposed to be funny?"

"Actually, yes, but I'm thinking of getting some new material."

"Why don't you think about leaving me alone? I'm not in the mood."

"It wasn't real, you know, Cal. Stromfeld, the bombs, what we did or didn't do. Don't let it get you down. It's just a training program. Nothing about it was real."

"But it could be." There was hurt in Cally's eyes, and shock, and confusion. "One day it could be, couldn't it? We're training now because if we ever pass the course one day we'll be doing this for real. Stromfelds exist, don't they? Madmen and their crazy schemes. One day real lives might well depend on us. And what happens then?"

"Then? Then we'll get it right," said Eddie. "I hope."

CHAPTER TWO

Before . . .

IGC DATA FILE DTC 7046

. . . stands on edge of disaster. According to the Nostradamus Trust, a leading global thinktank, the earth is about to enter a period of crisis as great as any in its history.

"Everywhere we look," says Dr. Abu El Sharif, the organization's chairman, "we see conflict and the seeds of conflict. Law and order in many regions of the planet are collapsing, with terrorist groups only too willing to exploit the resultant anarchy. Technology is spiraling out of control, the barriers too often down between what Man can do and what he ought to do. Multinational corporations wield more influence than many countries. A new elite is emerging of mega-rich, powerful men, an elite that thinks itself beyond the rules and regulations that govern the masses. Global stability is threatened in any number of ways as we enter the 2060s, and unless someone makes a stand, takes a lead – someone of vision and passion – the Nostradamus Trust sees nothing ahead for Mankind but apocalypse. . . ."

Senior Tutor Elmore Grant sighed and ran his hands through his worryingly graying hair. It was a gesture he allowed himself only when sitting alone in his darkened study at Spy High, as he was now. He supposed he ought to turn the lights on, though he'd spent so much time in his study over the years that he could negotiate it blindfolded. Besides, darkness helped him think, and tonight he needed to think.

Not many hours earlier he'd had Bond Team facing him from the opposite side of his desk, or not facing him, to be more precise; not daring to look their tutor in the eye, hanging their heads in shame. As well they should. He'd read to them the results of the first-year teams' latest exposure to the Stromfeld program: "Solo Team: pass. Hannay Team: pass. Palmer Team: pass. Bond Team . . ." He hadn't needed to say any more. Of all four groups of students, Bond Team was the only one to have failed the test. Bad enough. Dangerous enough for their future chances of survival. But what made the situation worse for Grant was that, of all four groups of students admitted to Spy High that year, Bond Team was the only one he'd personally selected.

Where had he gone wrong? Was he losing his touch, getting too old?

As if to emphasize the possibility, his legs started to ache. They did that sometimes, usually in the bleakest and loneliest moments of the night, and quite inexplicably, bearing in mind that a terrorist bomb caused Senior Tutor Elmore Grant and his original pair of legs to part company some twenty years ago. The limbs that held him up now were fashioned by craftsmen from synthetic bones and skin grown in labs. They couldn't ache. They couldn't feel anything. The tingling sensation he was experiencing now was psychological, not physical, a distant echo of the days when he'd been a whole man. The days when *he'd* been the secret agent, the spy, risking his life for the greater good. Not the has-been who sat in his study and picked raw teenagers to do the job for him.

Grant clicked on his desk lamp, casting an arc of yellow light across the files belonging to the members of Bond Team. Six students stared up at him from their first day photographs. How much a trained eye could tell about them, even from a single pose, a second immortalized by the camera. Eddie Nelligan, red hair deliberately uncombed, grin too wide, tongue almost protruding, pretending to be mocking the whole process, but in his eyes, kept sheltered and shielded, a steely determination. Cally Cross, the only African American in the group, wearing her dreadlocks proudly, like a badge of defiance, but also uncertain, untrusting, not quite looking at the camera in case she should see herself as she really was. Lori Angel, with the face of one, too, a tide of blonde hair, the china-blue eyes of a doll, yet her smile seemed on the brink of tears. Jennifer Chen, reckless, impatient, scarcely capable of stillness, driven by the secret that she would not share. And then Jake and Ben.

Grant permitted himself a second sigh, as if they were rationed and had to be used sparingly. He picked up the photos of the two boys, weighed them in his hands, compared them. Jake, brooding, intense, uncompromising, crackling with energy even in two dimensions. Ben, arrogant, aloof, aristocratic, certain of himself and his place in the world. Jake's unruly black hair to Ben's regimented blond. Opposites. Opposites intended to work together. The perfect balance — that had been Grant's plan. Only the plan didn't seem to be working. So far between Jake and Ben it was all conflict and no cooperation. Maybe he'd been too optimistic. Maybe the two of them would never gel.

Maybe Ben would never gel with anyone.

Grant recalled the reports that had drifted to Spy High from their Selector Agent network on the East Coast, messages that concerned one Stanton, Benjamin T., heir to the Stanton banking fortune but notable for more than his money. A brilliant mind. An outstanding athlete. A potential asset to the cause. Grant had placed a Selector on the staff of Ben's school to monitor him and report back. Those reports had been glowing, with one reservation: arrogance. Ben was good, but he knew he was good. *Might not be a team player,* the reports concluded.

Grant had decided to see for himself . . .

IGC DATA FILE DVG 7II3

. . . calls for brain-booster implants to be banned after mathematics prodigy Oliver Harcourt-Evans, five, suffered a seizure while delivering a lecture in quantum mechanics at Blair College, Oxford. Rumors that the boy genius's frontal lobes melted after booster surgery on his brain are at present unconfirmed. . . .

This was his moment.

When they made a film of his life (and sooner or later they would, he was certain), this shot would be in it. Benjamin T. Stanton Jr. taking his rightful place at the center of attention, the football in his hand, the score even, seconds to go. The crowd holding its collective breath as the opposition defense bore down like human tanks on Upstate High's star quarterback, the teenage prodigy of school sport. What should he do? The moment hung on his decision. And he was reveling in it. He was laughing.

Wide receiver available to his right. Ben could throw the ball. He trusted himself that the pass would connect. But if he did that, the center of attention would shift, the gaze of the crowd would switch. He'd be relegated to making up the numbers as Willie Liebowitz charged for touchdown.

Ben wouldn't stand for that. If anyone was going to win the game for Upstate, he was.

He ran. A rush for glory as the seconds ticked by. He clutched the football close to his chest, as vital as his heart. He darted past the first flailing arms of the defense. They were stupid, slow. He could outrace them all. The clamor and cries of the crowd spurred him on. Groping hands, desperate lunges. He was like lightning, like quicksilver. No one could stop him. Frantic fingers scraped at his heel but he was beyond them. He was alone. The line was there for him to cross. He thrust the ball upward like the Olympic torch.

Touchdown.

His teammates were around him then, pressing close, hailing, hooting, hauling him onto their shoulders. Ben accepted their adulation, punched the air in triumph so hard he might have left a bruise. He tugged off his helmet so that he could be admired more easily and looked to the crowd. Every one of them was cheering him, acclaiming him, every last . . .

Except one man. One man remained motionless in his seat while all around him people were standing, surging forward. He stood out like a mourner at a wedding. His arms were crossed defensively, as though he refused to be impressed. He was staring directly at Ben, and his expression was mocking. Ben found himself wondering who he was, why he wasn't joining in the general celebration. He had the time only to absorb that the man was gray-haired and middle-aged before his teammates wheeled and paraded him over to the other side of the grounds. What did it matter, anyway? He'd never see the man again.

Only the man was waiting for him when he left the changing room.

"Benjamin T. Stanton Jr.," he said, like he was ordering from a menu.

"That's me. You want something?"

"Possibly."

"You were at the game, weren't you? You a journalist or

something? Local paper? You want an interview? I can give interviews." It was disconcerting. The man didn't seem to need to blink. He stared at Ben as if examining a specimen on a slide.

"No, I'm not a journalist."

"Well, so?" Ben felt himself growing nervous. "Why are you looking at me like that?"

"I wasn't impressed, you know."

"What?" Maybe he was just a crazy, a weirdo. Maybe Ben was about to gain his very own stalker, and while that was something of a necessary fashion accessory in the celebrity world these days, Ben felt he'd sooner bring this strange conversation to an end. The tumbling exit from the changing rooms of some of his friends gave him an opportunity. They called to him, waved to him. There was Willie Liebowitz's party to go to, and Della Carey would be there with her elastic lips. And Della Carey had a thing about star quarterbacks who scored winning touchdowns in the dying seconds of a game. "Look," Ben said relievedly, "nice to meet you but I've got to go. Friends waiting . . ."

"It's a team game."

"Pardon me?"

"You could have passed the ball. You should have passed the ball. It's a team game. I wasn't impressed."

"What are you, some sort of coach?" His friends were still calling him, but they seemed distant now, unimportant. Ben was affronted. "I scored the touchdown, didn't I? I won the game."

"For yourself. Not for the team. There's a difference."

"The only difference is between winning and losing."

"If you think that, Benjamin T. Stanton Jr.," said the man, "then you certainly had better go with your friends. Be a big fish in a small pond. For the rest of your life."

"Hey," protested Ben, "what gives you the right to talk to me like that?"

His friends were calling him, their voices drifting away. "Ben, let's go! Willie's party! Della won't wait!" Leaving him behind.

"I know what's ahead of you, Ben," the man said, more sincerely now, more urgently, as if his time were running out. "A scholarship to Harvard. A partnership in your father's law firm. Plenty of wild oats and then marriage to a sweet-smiling society hostess who never had an original idea in her life. Wealth. Position. Respectability. Benjamin T. Stanton III. A big fish in a small pond. Predictability, Ben. Tedium."

"So? Who are you?"

"I can offer you something more. Greater risks, yes, but greater rewards."

"I don't —"

"Have you heard of Deveraux Academy?"

"Deveraux . . . of course. I've heard my dad discuss it. Exclusive's not the word. What, you mean you have something to do with Deveraux Academy?"

"Devreaux Academy has something to do with me," said the man, "and it could have something to do with you, too." He produced a card and offered it to Ben. There was a single videophone number on it. "If you have the courage, take the card. If you have the courage, call the number."

Ben hesitated. When they made a film of his life (and sooner or later they would, he was certain), would this shot be in it, too? Taking the card from the mysterious stranger, committing himself to the unknown. Perhaps he'd been wrong before. Perhaps this was his moment now.

A final yell from his friends. Ben instinctively turned toward them.

"We'll meet again, Benjamin T. Stanton Jr."

And when he turned back, the gray-haired man was gone.

IGC DATA FILE DVM 7192

. . . damage to the Eiffel Tower after the recent terrorist attack is not as serious as was first feared, though visitors will not be permitted to climb the structure for many weeks yet. "Perhaps it is time to think about a force field," a French government spokesperson has suggested. "Our great public monuments must be protected and preserved for the sake of future generations." The anti-heritage group Past Caring has admitted responsibility for the outrage, the latest in a series of assaults on landmarks throughout Europe. . . .

Ben's message was waiting when Grant returned to Spy High.

As was one other, from a Selector in the midwest, Domer country, who was presently masquerading as a farmer. What the man had done to deserve that particular assignment, Grant could not imagine. It was the shortest of short straws. Nothing ever happened in the domes apart from the planting, growing, and harvesting of crops. No student at Spy High had ever been recruited from there. But there was a first time for everything, Grant reminded himself. Prejudice clouded the judgment and weakened the mind.

He focused his full attention on the dossier that the Selector had sent him. Subject's name: Jake Daly. The next day, Grant was on his way to the domes.

They were a breathtaking sight, he had to concede, sprouting to the skies like glistening glass mushrooms. The domes were the American government's response to the Great Contamination of the 2020s, when pollution levels had spiraled so high that much of the country's food supply had been tainted. From the chaos of food riots and widespread social unrest that had followed, the domes had risen as a symbol of order and stability, safeguarding tens of miles of prime agricultural land — endless expanses of wheat rippling in the gentle breezes of the perfectly controlled environment, a guarantee of full bellies for all.

Which was fine, of course, unless you happened to live there. Some people, those who worked the soil, spent their entire existence beneath the sheltering structures, never feeling too hot or too cold, never feeling rain, never seeing a storm. Children were born and raised there, never knowing anything else. Most Domers, even the young, seemed happy with their lot, contented.

Jake Daly wasn't one of them.

A rebel, the dossier said. A nonattender at school only because he had already learned more than the undertrained staff could teach. Quick to pick fights with visitors to the dome, outsiders, tourists with cameras who liked to pose with pretty little Domer children and then go back to the cities and the Real World. A powder keg of potential that would be shamefully squandered if, by accident of birth, Jake was doomed to remain a Domer.

Grant didn't have to go far to find him. He browsed the streets of the Border Zone, the shantytown that had evolved at the dome's checkpoint, and followed the sounds of brawling.

There were two of them on him, bigger than Jake, older. Their clothes would normally have denoted wealth, fashions beyond the aspirations of Domers, although the effect was spoiled a little by their coating in dust and the occasional tear.

The designers probably hadn't deliberately gone for the blood-stained effect, either. Jake's jeans and simple white shirt were unblemished.

Grant could see why. He was powerfully built and fought like a natural, instinctive and deliberate. Where his opponents flailed and swung their fists wildly, Jake jabbed and struck with neatness and precision, outmaneuvering each attack with ease. Grant wondered how Jake would perform on the hologym combat programs back at Spy High. Certainly, they ought to provide more of a challenge than his present workout.

The two outsiders were groveling on their knees. They'd had enough. Black eyes rather than white flags were their sign of surrender.

"Ready to go now?" Jake asked with mocking politeness.

"Yeah, you win," groaned the first outsider, checking that his teeth were all present and unbroken. "We'll go."

"That's good," said Jake. "And the next time you rich boys feel like you want a good laugh at someone else's expense, try somewhere else."

"Yeah, right. At least we *can* go somewhere else," the second outsider taunted. "You're stuck in this hole for the rest of your life. Think about that, Domer."

Bleakly, Jake watched the beaten youths hobble away. "Don't remind me," he muttered, thinking there was nobody to hear.

"It doesn't have to be that way."

With a start Jake saw Grant for the first time. "Who're you?" he snapped defensively.

"Tell me, Jake, have you ever heard of Deveraux Academy?"

* * *

When he returned to Spy High, Grant made a note to reassign the Dome Selector to another location, maybe the Caribbean. By way of thanks.

His new team now numbered two.

IGC DATA FILE DV0 7214

. . . the escape of no fewer than thirty hardened criminals from the Aquatraz Undersea Maximum Security Prison. Police forces in the nearest coastal towns are on full alert. The authorities are shocked by the scale of the breakout, and inside help is suspected. "Something fishy's going on," said a spokesperson. Meanwhile, the resignation of Prison Governor . . .

There'd been slight problems with Jake's parents, particularly the father, for whom a son in the fields saved a farmhand's wages, but they both consented to Jake's departure for Deveraux in the end, however grudgingly. The academy's emphasis on offering places only to the "extraordinarily gifted" probably clinched it, as it usually did. Parents liked to believe their children were special. Whatever the reason, the Dalys signed the appropriate forms without Grant having to resort to the hypnospray, though he would have done so if necessary. Hypnotic suggestion was a last resort only, but it had been used. The needs of Spy High and the safety of the world outweighed family considerations.

So Ben and Jake were signed up, but that was only part of it. Making them work, making them function as secret agents, that was what really mattered. A tip from a Selector identifying a teenage prodigy with one-liners as sharp as his racing skills led Grant to add Eddie Nelligan to the mix. The hope was that Eddie's sense of humor might create a kind of buffer zone between Ben and Jake's particular brands of intensity. So far, unfortunately, it hadn't happened. In today's Stromfeld program, for example, Ben had jeopardized the mission by not following orders and trying to reach the core before Jake as a matter of personal pride. Jake had then compounded the disaster by contradicting Ben over the defusing of the bomb, when the team leader had been right all along.

It wasn't good. For Bond Team, the clock was ticking.

But had he done any better in his selection of the female members? Maybe it was wrong of him to place too much blame on just Ben and Jake. Maybe he should be looking closer to home. A Spy High team ought to be as tightly knit as a family: Bond Team was currently making the Simpsons look like the Brady Bunch, and who had been responsible for casting?

Grant thought about Cally. Maybe their first meeting in a police station had been a sign of things to come.

IGC DATA FILE DVQ 7235

". . . fertile recruiting grounds for gangs, cults, and terrorist groups," Professor Landon continued. "Immediate action has to be taken to provide accommodation and education for these young people before it's too late. I know of some projects that teach computer skills to the homeless, granting them access to the latest technology, but these projects are too often underfunded and overlooked. The time has come . . ."

Cally sat sullenly in the interview room. Her face was set defensively, defiantly. Her years on the street had made her wary and suspicious. They'd also made her a criminal.

"You another cop?" she wanted to know as Grant entered.

"No, I'm not another cop."

"You my lawyer, then? 'Cause I'm not talking to nobody until I get a lawyer here. I know you cops got quotas to fill and I bet you can't wait to use me to help fill 'em. I bet I'm gonna be a real asset to your list of black female juvenile delinquents, right?"

"I told you I'm not a cop," said Grant quietly, "and I'm not a lawyer, either."

"What are you, then? A tourist? Wait. Don't tell me — you're some sort of Jesus freak. Well, me and my soul are doing fine on our own, thanks."

"No, none of those." Grant sat down opposite Cally and regarded her thoughtfully. "I'm your ticket out of here."

"What? You're gonna get those rich folks to drop the charges? You got more chance of running into Elvis on the way home." But there was a note of hope in Cally's voice, nevertheless.

"I don't just mean out of this police station," Grant said. "I mean out of your whole way of life."

"What are you talking about? Who are you?" But she was sitting forward, the cold mask melting.

"Where's your family, Cally?"

Now there was pain in her eyes, a hurt that nobody could keep hidden, even if they were older and harder than Cally Cross. "Nowhere near me, that's for sure. 'Course, I must have had parents, right? Everybody does. But mine, I guess they must have got a better offer somewhere else. Can't think why, can you? Most folks'd love to have a daughter about to do time at the tender age of fourteen, wouldn't they? Hey, you're not my dad, are you . . . ? Nah, guess the color thing's a bit of a problem."

"So you've lived on the street your whole life."

"You asking me or telling me?" Cally shrugged, as if it didn't matter. "As long as I can remember."

"Education?"

"I learned a few things. A woman in a shelter taught me to

read. Real useful skill when you're homeless and hungry. But I got by — I get by. I catch on quickly."

"So where did you learn to make this?" Grant produced a small electronic device and placed it on the table between them.

"Cham!" Cally snatched it up and stroked it like a pet. "I wondered what they'd done with you."

"What did you call it?"

"Cham," Cally said with a grin, apparently forgetting where she was and why she was there. "As in 'chameleon.' This is my chameleon unit."

"Is that right? Mind explaining what it does?"

"Do I get time off for good behavior if I do?" Grant's face expressed no emotion. Cally shrugged. "Okay, why not? What you do with little Cham, here, is you attach him to a household alarm and he blends right on in, just like a chameleon disguising himself. He fools the alarm into thinking he's a part of the same system and that everything's nice and normal, but all the while he's breaking the circuit so me and my friends can sneak into rich people's houses and give their insurers one heck of a headache. Works every time. Worked this time."

"Trouble was, this time one of your so-called friends turned out to be a chameleon too, didn't they? Something they weren't? Sold you out for money."

"You can't trust people." Cally tried to say it lightly, but she didn't sound quite convincing. "People always let you down in the end. That's why I prefer computers, electronics, my little buddy Cham here. Computers you can trust."

"You obviously have a natural flair for such things."

"A girl can't spend her whole day begging for scraps on the street."

"How would you like to spend your whole day working on state-of-the-art computers, the latest software, virtual reality programs? Designing handy little gadgets like Cham, there?"

"Now I know who you are," scoffed Cally. "And I thought Walt Disney was dead."

"This isn't a joke, Cally," Grant said. "And I know a little more about you than you may think." Spy High even had Selector Agents on the streets, in hostels. No stone was left unturned for the right kind of recruit. "Enough to know that you can't be happy with the life you're leading now. Enough to know that behind the streetwise front, you're intelligent enough to take an opportunity when it's offered. What do you say? Interested?"

There was something in the man's voice that made Cally think of a father, a father she'd never known or loved or hugged. She stared hard at the table, didn't dare to look at the man directly. The chameleon unit was cold in her hand.

"How do I know I can trust you?"

"How do you know that you can't?"

Of course, in the end Cally had trusted him. She was at Spy High now. And, given how traumatized she seemed to be after this latest encounter with the Stromfeld program, maybe she'd been wrong to. Maybe Grant had been wrong to involve her. Maybe she was safer on the street after all.

Lori was struggling to find herself a little as well, and *her* background was about as impeccable as Ben's. Her face and form said beauty queen; her academic record said genius — almost off the scale. And she'd been so keen to join up, to do something to prove once and for all, to herself and to everyone else, that Lori Angel was more than just a pretty face, that she possessed abilities beyond her appearance. Yet Lori was the first and only one of the girls to find a steady boyfriend. Grant wondered whether that was irony.

As for Jennifer Chen, the Agent who'd described her had not exaggerated. She was without doubt the most talented martial artist for her age that anyone at Spy High had seen. It was the baggage that came with the skills that jeopardized Jennifer's progress — her own dark memories. Grant had gambled that the girl would gradually, eventually overcome these. But gradually, eventually seemed to be taking a longer time than he'd envisaged, and a gamble lost in the world of espionage could have dire consequences.

Grant leaned back in his chair and closed his eyes. He ran his hands through his hair. It was no use tormenting himself. It was not productive. He'd chosen Bond Team in good faith, on the evidence of their abilities as reported by respected Agents. He'd brought them here, yes, but what they did after arrival, how they coped was their own responsibility.

And there'd been fireworks from day one . . .

IGC DATA FILE DVS 7290

. . . witness Cherilee Fox described it as the most terrible sight she'd ever seen. "They were all so young," she said, "all so pretty. They should have had their whole lives to look forward to. And they were all singing there in the park and holding hands in like a big circle and then they all just kind of looked up to the sky and burst into flames. One minute they were flesh and blood, the next they were fireballs. What kind of world are we making here? I mean, what makes kids want to do something like that?"

The dead are all thought to be members of a suicide cult. Their names . . .

CHAPTER THREE

IGC DATA FILE DWW I400

... complete withdrawal from public life. The various companies, foundations, and institutions owned or sponsored by Deveraux continue to go from strength to strength, but Mr. Jonathan Deveraux himself, the ninth richest man in the world, has not been seen now for fifteen years. A debilitating illness has long been suspected as the reason for the multibillionaire's reclusiveness, though some say Deveraux now lives as a hermit, repenting the ruthlessness that once characterized his business dealings and drove many of his rivals to ruin. Exactly where Jonathan Deveraux is, however, and what he is doing to occupy his time, no one knows for ...

"Sorry, is this right?" Eddie squinted out of the cab window. Trees, more trees, and still more trees. "I mean, unless the maple syrup I poured on my pancakes this morning was hallucinogenic, I did see a nameplate for Deveraux Academy, and we did drive through a sort of gateway about ten minutes ago, but I just don't seem to see any sign of the actual school."

"The grounds," supplied the cabbie, "are extensive."

"Extensive? I've seen smaller countries. We go on much farther and we'll be changing time zones."

"Not much farther," said the cabbie. "Relax. Enjoy the ride."

"That's easy for you to say. You didn't have one cup of coffee too many before we set out."

But the cabbie was right. Eddie needed to chill out a bit and enjoy the moment. It was a moment he thought would never come, not even when Grant turned up that day at the SkyBike circuit. But here it was, the chance to immortalize the Nelligan name for the first time in history.

To be fair, Nelligans *had* been involved in pivotal world events of the past, at least according to family legend. There'd apparently been a Nelligan at the Alamo, which probably explained why Eddie wasn't keen on Mexican food. And there'd been a Nelligan with Custer at the Little Big Horn, too, an ancestor who was probably now wishing he'd called in sick that day. There was a Nelligan on the *Titanic*: third-class ticket, first-class view of the bottom of the Atlantic Ocean. And that was as far as Eddie had ever inquired into his heritage (he could see a trend developing that suggested he needn't worry unduly about pension funds). But the worst thing was, historians had never noted the Nelligan presence at these blockbuster-movie-friendly moments. Eddie's forebears never seemed to have been granted that big close-up. They always seemed to be the friend of the right-hand man of the right-hand man of somebody famous.

Well, that was something Eddie was determined to change. Spy High had an intake of just twenty-four students a year. That meant plenty of airtime for them all, Mrs. Nelligan's only son included. It was just a pity that the whole operation was so hush-hush, such a "Ssh! You-mustn't-breathe-a-word-of-the-true-purpose-of-Deveraux-Academy-to-anyone,-not-even-your-parents,-on-pain-of-death" sort of thing. Eddie reckoned there'd be more girls who'd look at him with more adoring eyes and more parted lips than usual if they knew what he was truly training for. He supposed he could always write his memoirs after graduation. Assuming he ever got that far. Right now it was fifty-fifty he'd even get as far as the school itself.

As if deciding to take pity on the complaining Eddie, the

woodland suddenly fell away, replaced by a more open environment. A lake in the distance. Was that a golf course? Gardens and lawns. A gazebo. Toward the horizon, sports fields, athletics tracks, buildings. And the biggest of these, the road finally, reluctantly winding toward it, Deveraux Academy itself.

It thrust into the air proudly, imposingly, towering over every other construction, dominating the skyline, its two wings flanking a gravel courtyard. The school's main entrance flung wide open, as if with greeting. Eddie marveled. It was like a Gothic mansion from several centuries ago had been miraculously transported into the present, bristling with buttresses, adorned with arcane sculptures, gargoyles, demons (not recent graduates, he hoped). He half expected to see a bell tower, complete with Quasimodo dangling from a rope. Gable rooms jutted from rooftops crazily sloped and slanted. Tall, austere leaded windows lined themselves up to look at the new arrival like disapproving maiden aunts. It was a building that promised hidden rooms and secret passages, damp cellars and dark adventure. Eddie grinned. Deveraux Academy did shelter certain secrets, he already knew that, and not everything was as it seemed, but the reality had little to do with ghouls, goblins, or madwomen kept in attics.

"Here we are," said the cabbie unnecessarily, pulling up outside a pair of forbidding oak doors. Probably Eddie's cue to pay him. The academy had sent Eddie money for his travel expenses. He could afford to tip big. On the other hand, you never knew when a little extra cash might come in handy.

The cabbie did not look happy as he drove away.

Eddie watched him go, then let his gaze drift to the right, where in the near distance a football game was in progress. Nothing unusual about that. Football was featured in every school's curriculum. A competitive game it was, too, each play hotly contested, both teams pressing hard. Nothing unusual about that, either. Yet something didn't quite fit. Something was wrong.

It suddenly occurred to Eddie what it was. No sound. No shouts from one player to another, no crunch of the collision of bodies, no umpire's whistle. It was like watching the ball game on TV with the volume turned off. Eddie frowned. Of course, the rational explanation was that the wind was snatching the sound away from him like a pickpocket's fingers. Only there wasn't any wind. He could still hear the cab quite clearly, and that was now almost out of sight.

Well, what did it matter? Maybe maintaining silence during competitive sport was part of a successful spy's training here at the college. Eddie picked up his bags and turned to face the doors.

Which swung open automatically.

If Bela Lugosi had appeared in a cape at the entrance and greeted him with a "Welcome to my house! Enter freely and of your own will!" Eddie would not have been unduly surprised, but nobody came. Instead, he stepped inside and found himself in a small foyer area, oak-paneled corridors leading off in either direction and a reception desk in front of him. The receptionist, a wizened little woman who seemed about as old as the building itself, regarded him with eyes as sharp as scalpels.

Eddie put down his bags. "Hi, my name's —"

"You'll have to work on that belly of yours," the receptionist observed, indicating Eddie's offending midriff with a withered finger.

"Pardon me?"

"You're out of condition, young man. Too soft, that's your problem. I'm surprised we've got any suitable students here at all these days." The receptionist shook her head sadly.

"Um, is this a school or an aerobics class?" The day was getting stranger. "Or are you talking in some sort of code?"

"Do you know, in my day I could have killed you in seven different ways without leaving my chair."

"Ah . . . in Venice the streets are full of water. The nights are cold in Moscow." Eddie wasn't doing well. "May the force be with you."

"Mr. Nelligan, isn't it?"

"Psychic as well," Eddie muttered.

"Take a seat, please, Mr. Nelligan. Senior Tutor Grant will be along in a moment." The receptionist sniffed. "He must have been having a bad day."

"Thanks," said Eddie. "It's been, er, fun."

Stooping low to retrieve his bags, he glanced for the seating that the receptionist had suggested was available. That was when he saw her. Or rather, saw her legs. Long, shapely, tightly encased in jeans. The kind of legs boys like to see. Eddie ogled.

"The rest of me's up a bit higher," the girl said, leaning forward, "or do you have some sort of neck problem?"

"No, no." *Pull yourself together, Nelligan*, Eddie thought. *Spy with a smile. Make an impression.* He grinned at the girl. "Bags are heavy. Thanks for asking."

She was gorgeous. Chinese American. Feline. The lithe, supple limbs and flashing green eyes of a cat. *Please, Lord*, Eddie prayed, *let her be in my group.*

"If I introduce myself," he said, "you're not going to welcome me to the academy and invite me to take a seat, are you?"

"Try me."

"Eddie Nelligan."

"Jennifer Chen. And these are my legs, since you seem so interested. Left and right."

"Hi, it's good to meet you, all three of you. Mind if I . . . ?" Eddie crossed to the cluster of chairs and chose one opposite Jennifer. "I've just arrived."

"You don't say. And I thought carrying those bags around was part of your fitness routine."

"Very good." Eddie laughed graciously. *Sarcastic as well as gorgeous. This one is going to be a challenge.* Eddie felt that he could rise to it. "What about you, Jennifer? Obviously not interviewing for any job requiring diplomacy skills."

"I imagine we're both here for the same reason," Jennifer said, without stating it. "Though if I'm kept sitting here any longer, I might have second thoughts and leave."

"Don't do that. We haven't gotten to know each other yet."

"You're right. Let's look on the bright side."

"Listen," Eddie said. "Maybe we'll get more sense out of someone our own age rather than the fossil behind the desk." A pair of students sauntered along the corridor toward him. A girl and a boy, leaning close together and laughing quietly, as if sharing some secret joke. Not seeming to notice Eddie. Not even when he addressed them directly. "Hi, my name's Eddie. Me and my friend are —" They strolled blithely past him. "Excuse me? Hello?"

"Do you normally have this effect on people?" Jennifer wanted to know, with a not altogether sympathetic laugh.

Eddie frowned, and for more reasons than his embarrassment in front of Jennifer. This wasn't right. It was like the silent ballgame. Nobody was so impolite as to totally ignore him, not even to acknowledge his existence. The frown led to anger. "Hey, I'm talking to you two." Eddie hastened after the oblivious students. He reached out his hand. "Are you listening . . ."

His hand went right through them.

". . . to me?"

The students continued on their way.

"Jennifer?" Eddie retreated, gazing at his hand as if it were something alien. "Did you see that?"

"Yeah, and I can see this as well." Eddie looked. Jennifer was on her feet and approaching another pair of students who were following in the same direction as the first. Indeed, they seemed to be identical to the first.

Jennifer stood in their path. They passed through her without a pause.

"Holograms," sighed the receptionist, as if Jennifer and Eddie should have known all along. "Everyone you see outside. Everyone you see on this level of the building, myself excepted, of course."

"Shame," muttered Eddie.

"The public face of Deveraux Academy. Of course, in my day we used to hire actors. Ah, well." The receptionist sighed nostalgically. "Senior Tutor Grant will see you now. And good luck to you both . . . you'll need it."

Grant was standing farther down the corridor. He beckoned for Eddie and Jennifer to join him. "It's all right. Leave your bags. Mrs. Crabtree will have them taken care of. Thank you, Mrs. Crabtree."

"Crabtree?" Eddie snorted, joining Grant. "That's got to be a code name, right?"

"Wrong. And speak the name with respect. Violet Crabtree is the oldest surviving former secret agent in the academy. We're very lucky to have her. But now to business. Come with me, please."

Grant opened a door into a room lined with books and occupied by a heavy mahogany desk. When all three of them were inside, he closed he door.

"Wow," admired Eddie. "Is this a study or a library?"

"Neither," said Grant. "It's an elevator."

"What?"

"Please," Grant indicated to Jennifer. "The door?"

"But we haven't —"

Eddie was glad to see Jennifer as bemused over Grant's instructions as he'd been over the holograms. She opened the door carefully. And they both gaped.

No corridor of oak now. The two teenagers stepped into a vast, pulsing room of metal, glass, and plastic. Banks of machinery hummed and whirred. Men and women in white coats sat at computers, caressing their keyboards like concert pianists. A battery of monitors circling the entire room displayed views of the world's major cities and monuments. Other screens presented live sound and pictures from what might have been every significant news network on the planet. The room throbbed with voices in countless languages, the gossip of the globe distilled.

"Do you get the Cartoon Network here?" Eddie asked.

"We get *everything* here."

"What's it all for?" Jennifer struggled to assimilate the barrage of sounds and images that assaulted her.

"We are now beneath the main academy building," explained Grant. "This is our IGC, our Intelligence Gathering Center.

Nothing happens on the earth today that we don't hear about as, or in most cases, *before* it happens. This room is the eyes and ears of our operation. It tells us where we're needed and why. This is the beginning of what Deveraux Academy is truly about." He rested his hands on the youngsters' shoulders. "Eddie Nelligan, Jennifer Chen. Welcome to Spy High."

IGC DATA FILE DVX 7537

. . . resigned after a series of failures to prevent terrorist attacks on high-profile targets, the latest being the Hovertel Disaster. "Our present law enforcement bodies are simply too slow to respond to the kind of threat that we face today," Constantine said. "We need a new kind of protection against society's enemies – a new breed of protector – and until that happens, we will always . . ."

It was a bit like being at a disco, Eddie thought, *although admittedly without the music, the flashing lights, or the girls scurrying off to the bathroom in pairs.* Spy High's new intake of students milled around with drinks or snacks in their hands, not quite certain of what to say or how to introduce themselves to their fellow wannabe secret agents. The color-coded name badges they'd been given as they entered the recreation room were obviously designed to make things easier. They'd certainly helped Eddie. When he and Jennifer had both received blue badges, he'd scarcely been able to restrain his enthusiasm: "Hey, what a coincidence. Looks like we're gonna be in the same group." Meaning: *You and me baby, you and me.* Jennifer's expression suggested that she'd recently swallowed a lemon.

Still, at least it gave him an excuse to follow her around all the time without being arrested. They'd also managed to locate the other four members of their group. Eddie wondered whether he ought to leave there and then and buy a lottery ticket. He couldn't believe his luck. As if Jennier's lissom charms were not enough for a poor red-blooded male, Lori Angel and Cally Cross hardly needed to think about plastic surgery either. Lori was a textbook blonde, while Cally's meticulously beaded dreadlocks lent her a more exotic kind of allure. All different, but all ravishing. Surely one of them had a soft spot for redheaded guys with Irish backgrounds.

Unfortunately, the two male members of the team weren't so promising. There was the tall blond guy, whom Eddie suspected was in the habit of carrying a mirror around so that he could admire himself whenever the urge took him, which was probably often. Ben Stanton Jr., he'd announced, like they should already have known (and did he really refer to himself as "junior"?). He seemed to regard everybody else as if they were a different, faintly uglier species, or might benefit from extinction at an early opportunity. Jake Daly, on the other hand, reminded Eddie of a wild animal primed to pounce. Eddie smiled a lot at Jake (although not *too* much). He didn't think he'd want him as an enemy.

They were still at the small-talk stage (so small it was virtually microscopic) when Grant clapped his hands and called for "some attention, please." He was clearly about to launch into some kind of speech. Eddie thought he'd hear it better if he was standing alongside Jennifer. Actually, if he was standing alongside Jennifer, who cared what Grant said anyway?

It had something to do with "the adventure" on which they'd just embarked. "From the moment you entered the door of Deveraux Academy," Grant pointed out, "your lives changed forever. From the moment you became students at this institution, a place previous graduates have amusingly but accurately rechristened Spy High, you turned your back on your previous existence and committed yourselves to a daring, dangerous future. Your training period at Spy High will be two years of constant challenge. You will be tested, tried, examined. Driven to your limits and beyond. And there will be no respite, no retreat, no place to hide. Not for one day, not for one moment. Many of you will have doubts; many will harbor a fear of failure. Some of you may even fall by the wayside and never graduate. It happens. At Spy High, only the strong survive, because only the strong can protect this nation and this world of ours from the dark forces that threaten to destroy it. But take courage. Never lose heart. None of you are here by coincidence. You all possess those skills and qualities that we think will equip you not only to cope with the demanding regime at Spy High, but also to transcend it, to excel, to achieve, to surpass those students who went before you." Grant paused. "You have been chosen as the best of the best." He paused again. "Prove us right."

There was applause. Ben Stanton (*junior*, Eddie reminded himself) seemed keen to lead it, although whether in approval of Grant's words or to congratulate himself for being there, Eddie couldn't be sure.

Grant raised his hands. "Tomorrow, Mr. Deveraux himself, our founder and the mastermind behind our work at Spy High, will address you and tell you more about your time here. For now, one last observation from me. Look around you. Look at those of your peers who are wearing the same color badge." Eddie didn't need to be told twice. He hoped a group hug might be in order. "They may just be names and faces to you at the moment —" *and the rest*, Eddie thought — "but these will be the most important people in your lives from this moment on. Your career, your success, your very survival at Spy High and beyond will depend, not only on yourselves, but on those people, too. You entered our school as individuals, but you will leave it as a team. Red for Solo. Gold for Hannay. Green for Palmer. And blue —" he instinctively held his breath — "blue for Bond."

Bond Team, Eddie mused. *Named after the greatest secret agent of them all. Apparently, they were following in James Bond's footsteps. How cool was that?*

"I hear there's some sort of inner-team competition over the year," Ben said after Grant had finished and the socializing resumed. "We'll have to win that."

Bond Team had split into two groups on the basis of gender. Eddie would have liked to have sidled over to the girls but judged that a little male solidarity might be more politic for the moment. He didn't want to give the impression he was only there for the flirting opportunities.

"Inter-team competition," Jake repeated skeptically. "Well, I hear we've got exams to pass at the end of this term first, and one problem at a time's enough for me."

"You've got to aim high, Jake," Ben said, with a slight trace of arrogance. "Think like a winner or end up a loser."

"Fortune cookies," observed Jake. "Don't you just love 'em?"

Ben regarded him more closely. "You're not a Boston Daly, are you?"

"A Boston Daly? Isn't that a newspaper?"

Sensing a disagreement brewing, Eddie intervened. Maybe he should have joined the girls, after all. "So where are you from, Jake?"

His reward for trying to keep the peace was a kind of what's-it-got-to-do-with-you glare from Jake. "Dome Thirteen, Oklahoma State," he replied grudgingly.

"Dome?" Ben said in half-pity, half-disgust. "You're a Domer?"

"You got a problem with that?" *Rich boy*, Jake was thinking.

Eddie was relieved that Ben quite mildly claimed not to have a problem, "with that" or anything else, though he suspected that Junior was going to be giving it some thought on his own time. He took advantage of the momentary silence to direct the conversation toward a topic that neither Ben nor Jake could possibly find controversial. "Hey, I wonder what the girls are talking about?"

"Don't worry, Eddie," Ben said. "It won't be you."

"They're all right, though, aren't they?" Eddie nudged his companions. "And enough to go around."

"You like your chances then, do you?" It seemed that even Jake could manage an expression roughly equating to vague amusement.

"Why not? Back home, I've got something of a reputation."

"That I can believe," Ben snorted.

"Okay, I'll bet you." Eddie's pride was stung. "I'll bet I can hook up with one of our fetching female teammates —"

"Only one?"

"Which one?"

"Any one. And, if you'll let me finish, I'll bet I can have her eating out of my hand within a week. Trust me." It was a foolish bet, Eddie knew, but at least it had united Ben and Jake.

"But Eddie," Ben pondered, "this eating out of your hand thing, do you mean literally?"

IGC DATA FILE DVZ 7541

. . . ratification of the Schneider Protocols to regulate the science of genetic engineering. "This is a major step forward," said U.S. Negotiator Emma Trabert. "There are too many rogue geneticists out there. The protocols are vital toward monitoring and restricting the kind of work that's going on. Who knows what might happen if genetics gets out of hand? I think we can safely say . . ."

"What do you think of the boys?" Lori asked, as she, Cally, and Jennifer unpacked their things and settled into their room. The girls shared a triple room in one part of Deveraux's accommodation wing, while the boys were similarly housed in another.

"I'm trying *not* to think of them," grunted Jennifer. "They're boys. You know what they'll be after. One-track minds, if they've got minds at all. Nothing but a distraction from why we're here. That Eddie's already winking at me every five minutes like he's got some sort of nervous twitch. If he's the best of the best like Grant said, the world's in worse trouble than we thought."

"I don't know," said Cally, thinking of Jake's strong, brooding features and his wild black hair that was just waiting for fingers to be run through it. "I don't think they're that bad."

"Well I think they're all right," Lori said, with a firmness that surprised herself. "I think we're lucky to have them on our team. I think they're nice."

"I expect the feeling will be mutual," noted Jennifer pointedly.

"Meaning?"

"Meaning, they'll think you're nice, too, Lori. What else?"

Lori frowned. She wasn't sure she liked Jennifer's implication. Her tone suggested that she wasn't taking Lori seriously, that she thought Lori was just there to look pretty, to find a secret agent for a boyfriend, and maybe to get captured and rescued a lot. Or was she being paranoid? Either way, Grant had chosen her, and she had every right to be here. She was going to be a success at Spy High, the best that she could be. Her first step, she reasoned, was to find out all she could about her new teammates, to build a positive team ethic. It shouldn't be too hard. They all had a mutual interest in working well together.

Lori turned her attention back to Jennifer, who was reverently placing a framed photograph at the head of her bed. It looked like a family photograph, a Chinese family — two smiling parents, two beaming children, a little boy, and a slightly older girl. The girl was probably nine or ten years old. She was certainly Jennifer Chen.

"Oh, what a lovely photograph," Lori said. She reached to pick it up. "May I?"

"No!" Jennifer snatched the photo, clutching it to her. Green fire in her eyes. Sudden and inexplicable rage.

"Okay, okay," Lori surrendered. "I only wanted to look. I wasn't going to tear it up or anything. Guess I can do without."

"What's going on?" asked Cally, concerned.

Jennifer glanced defensively from one roommate to the other and sensed that she'd made herself look foolish. "Sorry, sorry." She laughed without conviction. "It's just . . . this is the only photo of my family I have with me so it's, you know, important to me. I thought you might . . . if you dropped it or something. You know. Sorry."

"Don't worry about it," calmed Lori. "I shouldn't have made a grab for it. I'll know next time."

Jennifer smiled, and Lori smiled, too, but only on the surface. Maybe the positive team ethic might have to wait awhile.

IGC DATA FILE DVZ 7599

"Fear of the future is the single greatest source of anxiety for clients," company chairwoman Eleanor Croon declared to the delegates at the National Counselors 'R Us Conference in New Pittsburgh yesterday. "It's our job to make people feel safe again." Her speech was interrupted when a malfunctioning hoverbus smashed through the roof of the conference center, killing several delegates. Sabotage is suspected. . . .

CHAPTER FOUR

IGC DATA FILE DWB 7604

... theft of scientific equipment from the installation. The precise nature of the materials stolen has not been made public, but the involvement of U.S. Negotiator Emma Trabert in the investigation has led some to theorize that this mysterious affair is connected to illegal genetic experimentation. ...

"On land," said the voice of Jonathan Deveraux, and the great solar cities of the California coast surged up among the students like the peaks of shining mountains.

"At sea." And the deep oceans cascaded in and drowned them, their last sight being the underwater farms that harvested the produce of the seabeds.

"In the skies." They floated alongside the hovertels with their sports platforms prodding out high above the earth.

"And in the vastness of space itself." The United Nations moon colony appeared. Even though Cally knew she wasn't standing on the lunar surface in a vacuum, she still found it hard to breathe and was glad when Deveraux moved on.

"The history of mankind in the twenty-first century has been one of unparalleled advance and achievement." They could almost feel the pats on the back. "Yet there are dangers, too, in the world today. Threats to peace. Threats to order. Terrorists. Madmen. Megalomaniacs. Threats to our security of every kind."

And now the holographic scenes crashed together, and the solar cities burst into flames, the sea farms sabotaged, explosions in the air and silent screams in space. Mankind's dreams destroyed.

"Wow, wouldn't this make a great movie, guys?"

"Shut up, Eddie," said Ben.

The illusions faded. The face of Jonathan Deveraux regarded his students steadily from the screen before them. *It's like he can see inside us*, thought Lori, *like he's judging us, deciding if we're worthy. Mid-fifties*, she guessed, *handsome in an austere sort of way, with strong features that might have been molded from steel and eyes that glittered with purpose and conviction*. "It's God without the beard," Eddie had whispered earlier. Lori wondered if he might not be right.

"Who, then," Deveraux continued, "is best equipped to combat these threats, to stand strong, to stand tall, to battle and defeat the dangers that we face? Not the old — for the days of the older generation are done — but the young. It is the duty of the young to fight for our future, because the young *are* the future. You, my students. Each and every one of you. That is why you have been chosen. That is why you are here. Spy High was created to be a bastion of good against the forces of evil, a place where the young train to keep the world safe for tomorrow. It is an onerous responsibility that you have taken on your shoulders. Good luck."

"Luck?" said Eddie, as Deveraux vanished from the screen. "Who's gonna need luck? When the bad guys see Eddie Nelligan bearing down on them, they'll run a mile."

"Sure, Eddie," remarked Jennifer. "Why should they be different from everyone else?"

Bond Team laughed at that — Ben doing so rather quickly, to get it over with. These introductory sessions were all very well, but he wanted to move on. The dangers were out there, and he wanted to face them. He wanted a chance to prove himself.

"Hi." Another delay. Ben turned to see a youth several years older than them, perhaps nineteen, approaching with his hand outstretched. "You're the new Bond Team, right?"

"New?" Ben questioned.

"Well, this year's model." The youth grinned. "Thought I'd come over and say hello. Name's Will Challis. See, I was in Bond Team when I was training here. Team leader, in fact, although I think that was because no one else wanted the job."

Ben looked at Will Challis with genuine interest. A former leader of Bond Team. He'd already been where Ben wanted to go. Maybe this delay was going to be worthwhile.

Bond Team introduced themselves and shook hands.

"So, what, you're a graduate now?" Lori sounded impressed.

"That's right," Will Challis smiled. "Scroll and mortarboard at home. I keep them under the bed, right alongside my sleep-shot wristband and laser rifle."

"So you actually go on missions?" Eddie wanted everything clear. "Real missions?"

"Some," said Will Challis modestly.

"That must be great." Ben's eyes glazed as he imagined himself as Will Challis.

"By and large." Will's brow momentarily darkened.

"Can you give us an example?" Even Jake seemed struck by the presence of a live Spy High graduate. "Of a mission?"

"Well," considered Will, "do you remember the terrorists who hijacked that orbiting space station and threatened to crash it to earth unless their demands were met?"

"No." Bond Team looked at each other blankly.

"Of course not. That's because me and a team from Spy High rocketed up there, boarded the station, and overpowered the terrorists. No casualties of our own that time, either, which —"

"So what are you working on now, Will?" asked Lori. "Anything you can tell us about?"

"Well, there may be something in the works," Will said, "though I haven't been formally assigned yet. Even Spy High graduates work on a need-to-know basis, and I guess, so far I don't need to know. You can wish me luck, though."

"I doubt we're ever supposed to rely on luck," said Ben, "but if you want some extra help any time, look no further."

Will nodded his appreciation. "You deal with Stromfeld first, and I'll give it some thought."

"Who's Stromfeld?" quizzed Cally. "A teacher?"

"Kind of," Will reflected. "He'll teach you how little you know, all right. Stromfeld's what the college calls its principal virtual-reality training program. It's also the name of the main character in it — and that's gonna be the bane of your existence, let me tell you. You have to pass the program before the end of your first term, or the only mission you'll be going on is the one that's headed back to your old life. You get three attempts, though, because nobody expects a team to beat Stromfeld on the first try."

"We will," announced Ben.

Jerk, thought Jake.

"You're confident," said Will, "and confidence is good. But Stromfeld is a serious villain, a composite of every power-mad, humanity-hating, earth-coveting lunatic since Hitler. And the program's scenario is different every time. Your mission is always to defeat Stromfeld's avid plans for world domination, but those plans are never the same. And neither's Stromfeld. We've had bald Stromfelds, bearded Stromfelds, Stromfelds with metal claws, Stromfelds with clones. You never know what to expect." Will widened his eyes in mock horror. "And it's all waiting just for you. So I guess I'd better not keep you from your studies any longer. Good to meet you, Bond Team —" the handshaking recommenced — "and if you ever want a word, advice, anything, you only have to find me."

"We appreciate that, Will," said Ben. "Thanks."

They watched him leave.

"Do you think that'll be us one day?" Lori wondered.

"You know it," said Ben. *At the very least,* he thought, *it will be me.*

"Hey, Eddie," Jake noted, "you don't look too happy. The thought of Stromfeld upsetting you?"

"Stromfeld, no," said Eddie, "but did he say 'studies'? Don't tell me this is a school after all?"

IGC DATA FILE DWB 7845

. . . still searching for escaped techno-terrorist Sergei Boromov. With the notorious Pascal Z also on the loose, and with reports growing every day of increased activity within the anarchist and techno-terrorist community, the authorities fear that a number of outlawed groups may be beginning to work together. "The idea of a supercell of techno-anarchists combining their resources absolutely chills my blood," said Chief Investigating Officer . . .

Bond Team could forget about secret-agenting in the field for a while. To begin with, they could hardly find their way around the school, let alone a supervillain's secret complex. Gradually, though, everything began to fall into place. Above ground, in the gothic building that was the public face of Deveraux Academy, were the residential and some recreation rooms, as well as classrooms for those subjects on the traditional curriculum. "What?" Eddie had moaned. "We still have to take math? What good is algebra when you're being attacked by sharks? And English? Since when did Shakespeare save the world?" But there was no room for argument. And nobody wanted to argue when they ventured underground, in the study elevators. This was more like it. Here, hidden beneath the earth, was the high-tech training area of Spy High: the IGC, the virtual-reality chamber, the spycraft rooms, the hologym. Here, concealed from prying eyes, was where the real training took place.

The clothes they had to wear reflected their location. Above ground, and during school hours, the students wore the kind of smart and conservative uniform that might belong to any educational establishment. Below ground, they wore shock suits only. "And now I know why they're called that," Lori had complained. "They don't exactly leave anything to the imagination. Any tighter and I think I'd choke!" Eddie suggested that the girls keep them on at all times.

Then there were their teachers, a blur of names, and classes during their first few days. Grant himself, as their senior tutor, taught spycraft and the history of espionage. They obviously respected Grant, although the boys had been more immediately impressed by Ms. Bannon, their weapons instructor. *But then,* Lori reasoned sadly, *what teenage male wouldn't be taken with a tall, dark, very womanly woman whose first name was Lacey and who could strip down a laser rifle in thirty seconds flat?* Corporal Randolph Keene was in charge of disciplinary matters, tactical planning, infiltration techniques, and their general physical education. Their specific martial arts training was in the small but deadly hands of Mr.

Korita. "Is he really that short or is he actually sitting down?" Eddie had whispered during their first lesson. Ben had been equally dismissive: "What can a little guy like that teach us?" Until Mr. Korita had given his skeptical students an early indication of exactly what he could teach them by throwing Eddie and Ben over his shoulders. At the same time.

If only Eddie had learned from that, then an even more embarrassing incident might have been avoided during one of Mr. Korita's first lessons.

Lori could see that something was going on between the boys. There was a lot of whispering, a lot of nudging of Eddie's ribs by Ben and Jake, and a fair amount of Eddie nodding and grinning complacently, as if to suggest that whatever the situation, he was in control of it.

The lesson was in judo. Specifically, throws. Mr. Korita had already demonstrated the basic technique, and, as the bruises on Ben and Cally would testify, his hips were like hammers. Now it was his students' turn. Any volunteers? Jennifer, of course. Lori was quickly learning that if violence was involved, so was Jennifer. And who wanted to exercise their skills against Jennifer? Eddie, who never volunteered for anything except second helpings at mealtimes. Lori saw Jake and Ben sniggering. She saw momentary dismay on Jennifer's face harden into cold anger. Then they were gripping handfuls of each other's judogi jackets, planting their legs apart, bracing themselves. Then it started.

"Go on, Eddie, put your back into it!" The boys were laughing.

"Tip him, Jen! Knock some sense into him!" Cally obviously thought she needed to support the representative of her own sex.

Lori didn't cheer. Instead, she watched their faces. Eddie was doing well — surprisingly well, even — given that he never paid attention in class. He was standing firm, shifting his weight, apparently effortlessly, to compensate for every move Jennifer made to unbalance him. Lori could see her fury building, the green blaze in her eyes. Particularly as Eddie was still grinning nonchalantly, provocatively. And did he really say, "Shall we dance?"

But then he bobbed forward, whispered something inaudible in her ear, and compounded his transgressions with a peck on Jennifer's astonished cheek. She didn't take too kindly to that. With a cry of rage, which would have made Bruce Lee proud, Jennifer twisted her body, rammed her hip into Eddie's side like a runaway train and jerked him into the air. Eddie landed flat on his back, much to the hilarity of everybody.

"One down, two to go, Ed!" called Ben.

Even Mr. Korita allowed himself a meager twitch of the lips.

But not Jennifer. She was dropping on Eddie's chest, pinning him to the mat, winding his jacket around his neck like she was wringing a flannel, like she wasn't going to stop until she'd throttled him. "Don't ever try that again, you hear me? Not ever!" she yelled. And while most people were still laughing, Lori knew that she was serious and that it was only just within Jennifer's strength of will to obey Mr. Korita's injunction to let Eddie up. She had been very close to doing some real damage. Lori glanced across to the boys. Jake seemed to have sensed the truth, too, as he was regarding Jennifer with a new and more thoughtful interest, but Ben hadn't.

Jennifer was roundly applauded as she stood.

"So, Jen," groaned the prostrate Eddie, "is that a no, then?"

IGC DATA FILE DWE 7882

. . . latest in a series of disappearances in and around the Wildscape. Unlike the earlier missing persons, who were all tourists, Deke Pollock and Tolly Zane were local men, hunters, and they knew the area well. "No way could Deke and Tolly have just gone and got 'emselves lost," said Nathan Pardew, a friend of the missing men. "It's gotta be somethin' else. Somethin' out there . . ."

Ben thought about Will Challis a lot during those first weeks of term. Will: former leader of Bond Team. Ben: future leader of Bond Team. That was how he saw himself. Ben knew that he had it in himself to be the greatest graduate, the greatest secret agent Spy High would ever produce. He would never rest until he achieved that end. It was going to be his life's mission. But first, he needed to ensure his election as leader of Bond Team.

False modesty aside (and Ben was highly adept at putting false modesty aside), he didn't foresee much of a contest in that direction. Who was there in Bond Team who could match him? Cally Cross and Jake Daly he dismissed out of hand. A street urchin and a Domer. Far be it from him to doubt the quality of the Spy High selection procedure, but surely Grant could have found more promising material than those two. Admittedly, the girl looked like she had a bit of flair for computers, and he could see how that might be useful, but Daly's only talents seemed to be for surliness and slouching. He'd never be able to discipline himself. He'd never amount to anything outside a farm.

Eddie Nelligan was pretty much the same. Too fond of jokes and girls, although hardly successful with either. Nelligan would most likely turn the leadership of Bond Team down even if, by some perverse miracle, it was ever offered. He was a follower, and well behind the front rank. That left just Jennifer Chen and Lori Angel. Jennifer possessed the passion for leadership, Ben could tell, but not the self-control, while Lori was quietly accumulating an impressive string of test results in their various classes. Not quite good enough to overtake him, at least not yet, but sufficient for Ben to judge that it was Lori who could turn out to be his nearest challenger for team leadership.

And his early grades were outstanding, even if he did say so himself. Top of the year in spycraft and the history of espionage, full marks in physical training, undefeated in the hologym, star grades from Ms. Bannon and Mr. Korita. His credentials for the right to be leader had been emphatically established, and he felt that the others, with the ungrateful exceptions of Cally and Daly, were beginning to look at him with the appropriate respect. He felt that it was only a matter of time before he assumed his rightful role. Then they came to the SkyBikes.

SkyBikes emerged from the oil crisis that had virtually marked the end of private ownership of vehicles driven by the internal combustion engine. Environmentally friendly and operated by magnetic power, SkyBikes were like the more grandiose motorcycles of the late twentieth century, only without wheels and skimming several feet above the ground. As with all technological innovations, their price had initially been prohibitive, and until recently only the very wealthy had been able to afford them.

Ben had grown up with SkyBikes. His father had bought him his first machine for his fourth birthday, not that Ben was big enough to ride it then, but it looked good parked outside where visitors could see it. Ten years later and Ben could scarcely imagine that any of his teammates were more familiar with the capabilities of the SkyBike than himself. This was going to be another chance for him to shine.

And it certainly looked that way to begin with. As they sharpened their skills on the grounds of the college, Ben was pleased to note that Lori, Jennifer, and particularly Jake did not appear naturally gifted in this respect.

"Too bad it's not a tractor, eh, Jake?" Ben jibed. "I bet you'd come into your own then." Jake's answering glare made the day worthwhile.

On the other hand, though, Ben was surprised and slightly concerned to see that both Eddie and Cally could ride the skies like professionals. He vaguely remembered hearing that Eddie had a flair for racing, but surely Cally could never have afforded a SkyBike before. But they were fast, both of them, and slick in their turns, and they maneuvered their machines as if they were part of their own bodies. In the promised race that was to complete their first session, Ben could actually envision himself coming in third — an unthinkable underachievement. Something had to be done.

"You're pretty good on the bike, Eddie."

"Thanks, Ben. About time they gave us something I can do. I was beginning to think I'd been rechristened Eddie 'Last Place' Nelligan."

Polite laughter. "Cally's pretty good in the saddle, too."

"So I've heard."

"Could be your way in with her."

"How d'you mean?"

"Something in common. You get talking. You get smooching. You get a result."

"That's the way you work, is it, Ben?"

"All I'm saying is, you've obviously blown your chances with Jennifer. It's Cally or Lori. And you've already missed one deadline. If this bet of yours isn't going to turn into a major embarrassment . . ."

"Thank you for caring."

"Actually, I've got a bit of an idea, if you think you're up to it . . ."

It was a simple course, from one end of the grounds to the other, with only one real problem — the forested area toward the end, which would test the students' handling of their bikes to the limit.

Bond Team lined up at the start. Positions and times would be fed into the racers' aptitude scores, which were part of the data that students could access when it came time to elect the team leader. Ben smiled down the row of his teammates. Lori, uncertain. Jennifer, baffled. Jake, resentful. Cally, concentrating, at one with her machine. Eddie, acknowledging Ben with a nod. Ben gripped the handlebars more tightly. Third place was as bad as last place. He wasn't going to allow it.

Keene fired his gun. The SkyBikes roared into the air.

It swiftly fell into the pattern that Ben might have predicted. Even across open ground, he, Cally, and Eddie were able to coax a better performance from their machines than the others, breaking away, dividing the race into two. And as he'd feared, however hard he gunned the magnetic power core of his own bike, Eddie and Cally were leaving him behind, too, little by little.

They plunged into the forest with Eddie and Cally neck and neck. Ben tried to keep pace with them, to keep watching them, but now he also had to focus on the trees, or his race might come to a painful and premature end. And that wasn't in the plan. The SkyBikes streaked through the woodland, flashing, flitting from side to side like silverfish, to avoid collision. He wasn't gaining. He was losing ground.

It was down to Eddie now.

Eddie who had sped ahead, was leading Cally. In typical fashion, he couldn't resist glancing back over his shoulder and giving Cally a little wave. He couldn't, therefore, spot the tree that was looming steadfastly and solidly in front of him.

Cally saw it and screamed for Eddie to watch out.

Too late.

His SkyBike struck the tree a glancing blow, careered crazily groundward, skidded across the forest floor, and flung him from the saddle. He landed on his back and lay still.

"Eddie!" Cally veered off course, braked, and leaped to his side.

Ben accelerated ahead. *Third place?* he thought to himself. *Not likely now.*

Jake, next to approach the crash site, saw Eddie sprawled there, Cally kneeling over him, distraught. Cally was leaning close to him, her hands on him, her face all but touching his. And then Eddie, laughing, hooting, flinging his arms around her, and rolling them both across the grass.

"Eddie, get off me!"

"It's a miracle! I'm totally unhurt!"

"You won't be when I'm finished with you." Cally slapped Eddie with her hands. "You cheat! You fraud!"

Beneath the barrage of blows: "You say the nicest things, Cal. But come on, you were worried, weren't you? You care for me, don't you? Admit it. Now's the time."

"Never's the time for you and me, sleazebag." Cally got to her feet and stalked to her SkyBike.

"So then, a bit of mouth to mouth's out of the question?"

"Another first place," Jake said to Ben later, "even though Cally and Eddie are both better on the SkyBikes than you."

"That's not what the statistics say."

"Could have been a nasty accident, though, Eddie coming off his bike like that. I'm surprised you didn't see it happen, Ben, you weren't so far behind. But then, you couldn't have, could you, 'cause if you had, you'd have stopped, wouldn't you? Looking out for an injured teammate sort of thing. It's more important than winning a race, wouldn't you agree?"

"Eddie wasn't injured, Jake. He was just trying to score with Cally."

"Yeah. Funny way of going about it, though. I wonder where he got the idea?"

IGC DATA FILE DWF 7900 (ref. DWB 7604)

. . . surviving guard could only describe the intruders as "monsters, creatures that couldn't have been men" before he had to be sedated again. The authorities have dismissed such lurid claims as the ravings of a man in shock, though security has been further tightened both at Genetech and at other installations specializing in genetic research and experimentation. Since the Schneider Protocols . . .

CHAPTER FIVE

IGC Data File DWG 800

. . . latest fashion trend is designer eyes. The recipient's original eyeballs are removed and replaced by cybereyes in a range of fresh, bright colors. The new orbs are completely computerized and programmable to the customer's own specifications, so that they only see what they want to see. "These days, the world is a horrible place," said one potential buyer. "With cybereyes, I don't have to look at it any more." A special adults-only version, in which everyone appears naked, is still in development and . . .

The elections for team leader came at the end of the first month of term. Each student had one vote to award to anybody on their team, apart from themselves. The maximum number of votes that a student could accrue, therefore, was five, and Ben was expecting nothing less. If somebody didn't vote for him, with his record, then that somebody was allowing his or her judgment to be affected by selfishness and envy and obviously shouldn't be at Spy High in the first place.

Grant read the election results at the end of a spycraft lesson.

"Eddie Nelligan, one vote," said Grant dispassionately, as if it was all the same to him.

Eddie cried out, "I got a vote? Someone voted for me? I can't believe it!" The others patted him on the back like a pet dog who'd performed a trick. "That person is clearly in need of psychiatric attention and should be removed from school immediately. Why would anyone in their right mind vote for Eddie 'Last Place' Nelligan?"

Ben smiled inwardly.

"Jake Daly," Grant continued, as if he'd never spoken the name before, "one vote."

The backslapping now jumped to Jake, although Ben only joined in faintly. *Daly got a vote? Someone had rated a Domer more able to lead the team than me? Who was it? Who stabbed me in the back?*

"And finally," Grant concluded, "Ben Stanton, four votes." Whistles and applause followed and Ben struggled to appear modest. "Ben Stanton is therefore duly elected as team leader for Bond Team." But Grant could have sounded more excited about it, more impressed. He shook Ben's hand politely, as if he harbored reservations. Ben briefly toyed with the idea of reminding his tutor about big fish and small ponds but decided that now wasn't the time. He was aware of Lori's adoring gaze on him, her hand rubbing his back.

But four votes. Only four votes.

"Daly!" Ben grabbed Jake's arm as they left class. "Didn't you understand the rules?"

"What are you talking about?" Jake sighed, like a parent with a petulant child.

"The election. You weren't supposed to vote for yourself."

"What?" Jake bristled. "You think that just because you didn't win every available vote, I must have cheated? What, Ben, can't accept that someone out there might not share your belief that you're the greatest thing since Sherlock Holmes? Can't take a bit of competition?"

"You were supposed to vote for the best person for the job."

"So why aren't you talking to Eddie? How'd he get his vote?

Why accuse me?" As Ben's eyelids flickered, Jake realized the truth. "Oh, of course. Stanton, you really are something else."

"You voted for yourself because you resent me — resent my background."

"Listen, rich boy, true or otherwise, I'm not that petty. If you really want to know, I did vote for you. See, I can put the greater good before my personal feelings, but you know what? I'm already starting to regret it."

Ben frowned. "I don't believe you. So who voted for you?"

"I did," Cally said firmly, defiantly. "It was me."

Ben and Jake turned to regard her openmouthed with surprise.

"And do you want to know why? Because I think Jake would make a better leader, Ben, simple as that. You may be top of the class in your studies, but a million A-grades don't mean anything in the real world. You're a glory hunter. And I don't like you. And I didn't vote for you."

"Then it's just as well the others did." Ben launched an offensive. "Because if you want to know who's the real weakest link on Bond Team, street girl, just take a look in the mirror. If you can stand it."

"Nice one," Jake grunted. "Stanton, you're sure gonna be a winner for team morale."

But Ben didn't care. Team morale didn't matter. Only success mattered. And he was leader. They couldn't take that away from him. He'd gotten what he wanted.

IGC Data File DWG 8120

. . . trial of multibillionaire industrialist Maxwell Irons has collapsed. The flamboyant Irons, who once claimed that he was "untouchable" and "as far above the law as the eagle above the earth," is celebrating by holding a party for a thousand close friends at his ice ranch in Antarctica. The festivities are likely to last for at least a month, raising fears that the ecology of the area . . .

"Congratulations," said Will Challis.

"Thanks." Ben was sitting with Will in the rec room. "Looks like I'm following in your footsteps, then?"

"Looks like it. Well done, Ben."

"So does Deveraux have all of the team leaders in his room to congratulate them personally or something?"

Will regarded Ben pityingly. "Does Deveraux?! Let me tell you, Ben, it's been three years now since I've graduated, I've got successful missions in double figures, and I've *still* never seen our noble founder in the flesh. Neither has any student past or present that I've ever spoken to. Grant sees him, I know that. Grant is always being summoned to the inner sanctum for a head to head, I suppose it's a privilege of being senior tutor. But other than that, it's screens only. It's what you must have heard on the grapevine: Jonathan Deveraux is so reclusive he makes Howard Hughes look like a party animal."

"Howard who?"

"Don't worry. It's a twentieth-century thing."

So there was something else for Ben to aim for. The first student in living memory to set eyes on Jonathan Deveraux. Keep the idea warm for later. "Actually, though, Will, there was something I wanted to ask you. We've got our first attempt at the Stromfeld program coming up and, well, if you've got any tips . . ."

Will laughed. "He's the guy you should be asking, not me," he said, pointing.

"Who?" Ben turned in the direction indicated. Sitting facing the wall, but talking to it as though it was a trusted confidante, was a mummy of a man. His parchment skin was tugged so tautly across his bones that it seemed his skeleton was no longer prepared to wait for him to die but was making a push for liberation now.

"Gadge Newbolt," Will replied. "Gadge as in gadget, and Newbolt as in Professor Henry Newbolt, the mastermind behind the Stromfeld program and most of the school's other techno-marvels besides."

"Are you kidding?" Ben tried to restrain his skepticism. "How can that crazy old man be Professor Newbolt?"

"Who did you think it was? You must have seen him around."

"Wandering the corridors, yes," Ben admitted. "Talking to walls. I thought he was a janitor or something. I mean, I'd heard Professor Newbolt was a brilliant man."

"'Was' being the operative word," observed Will. "In his prime, Gadge was responsible for everything from the hologym to our finger bombs, nitronails. Have you had your session with those yet? They're little strips of plastic explosive that you stick on your fingernails and then when you need to, you rip them off, activating the fuse, stick 'em on another surface, and bang! A big hole. They come in handy, no pun intended."

"So what happened to Gadge?"

"I guess senility comes even to brilliant men," Will sighed. "The professor, he just started to lose it. His ideas became wilder.

Things like follicle fuses that you hid in your hair, only if you scratched your head too vigorously you could set them off, and then you'd be left with no hair and probably very little head. Detachable nipples that doubled as radio receivers. Didn't go down too well with Deveraux, apparently. So in the end, they phased him out. Early retirement. Oh, they still let him come and go as he pleases, but he's just tolerated now. Has a lab. Sleeps in it. Talks to walls, not people. Sad, really."

"So were you joking when you said I ought to be asking him for tips?"

"No wonder you're leader, Ben," grinned Will. "But I can give you some advice. In Stromfeld, expect the unexpected. And now I've got to go. Meeting with Grant. I think I might finally be getting my next assignment."

"Yeah? Well, good luck."

The two leaders of Bond Team shook hands.

"Thanks," said Will. "I'll see you around."

Off on a new mission, Ben mused enviously as he watched Will depart. One day. *One day.*

He finished his drink in a single gulp. There was a little mission of his own that he needed to carry out to make his day complete.

IGC Data File DWG 8185

. . . the so-called Extinction Hunts to be banned. "Killing one animal is a rush in itself," said one supporter of the hunts, "but to shoot down the last of an entire species, to wield that kind of power in your gun, that's worth paying any amount of money for. If only these protestor types would become extinct, the world would be a better place. In my opinion . . ."

Ben hadn't meant to eavesdrop on Lori and Eddie. But now that he was just outside her open door with the two of them inside — Lori sitting on her bed and Eddie pacing up and down with uncharacteristic nervousness — he wasn't just going to go away again. That was asking too much. Besides, what passed between Lori and Eddie now might have direct impact on his own plans, on what he was intending to say to Lori. So Ben listened.

"That's not true, Eddie, you're not a failure. Nobody thinks that."

"The computer does. The computer that ranks us all in order and reserves bottom place for me every time. It's like I've got a season ticket for sixth spot. You know what, Lori? I reckon that computer is a female, it's a girl, and that's why it's got it in for me. Girls don't like me, you know."

"That's not true either, Eddie."

Ben smirked. Eddie was changing tactics with Lori and playing the sympathy card. He doubted it would make any difference.

"I know it's hard to believe, but . . ."

"Impossible to believe. I mean, I like you."

"You do, Lori?" Ben could hardly suppress his laughter at the wide-eyed innocence in Eddie's tone. He'd move to the bed soon. "That makes me feel so much . . . nah, but you're just saying that."

"No, I mean it. I like you."

"Really?" The sound of springs. "Then that's good, 'cause I like you, too, Lori."

"Eddie!" More springs. Someone stood up. Lori's voice moved closer. "But not like that."

"No, of course not. I was just . . . you know, expressing gratitude. Your bed's kind of bouncy, if you know what I mean. I just kind of tipped over. . . ."

"Didn't you say you were on your way to the rec room?"

"That's right. That's right. It's that way, isn't it? Like, outside and take it right? Nice talking to you one on one, Lori."

"Bye, Eddie."

"Yeah. See you." Eddie rushed out of the room so quickly that he didn't even notice Ben. Muttering under his breath: "And in sixth spot in the category for success with the opposite sex . . ."

Ben controlled his amusement, set his features, and reminded himself of his reason for being here. Then knocked the door.

"Eddie, I thought you —" Lori opened the door more widely and was momentarily flustered when she saw who it was. "Ben. Oh."

"Is that an 'oh' as in 'carry on walking down the corridor, Ben, I'm washing my hair' or an 'oh' as in 'come on in, Ben, what a pleasant surprise'?"

"Come on in, Ben, what a pleasant surprise." First point in his favor. Second point in his favor: She closed the door behind him. "I'm Miss Popularity all of a sudden."

"Huh?"

"Nothing." Lori smiled. She had a dazzling smile. It would entrance anyone. Ben pictured that smile beside him. "Congratulations again, by the way, for being elected team leader. You'll make a good one, I'm sure."

"I'll certainly be trying," said Ben in his most self-effacing tone. "And congratulations to you, too, Lori."

"Me? Why?"

"I saw the scores. I might have come first, but not by much. And who came second? A quick clue to help the viewers at home: She's in the room."

Lori smiled again, blushing a little. It wasn't often people praised her for anything other than how pretty she looked in "that dress." "Bit of a mystery why nobody voted for me then, isn't it?"

"Well, people are sometimes blind to the obvious." Ben judged he could risk his next move. "But I'm not, though. My eyes are open. You can't hide your talents from me, Lori."

More color. Lori peeped bashfully at Ben from beneath her eyelids. "You'd better stop there, Ben. This is turning into a mutual admiration society."

"Is there something wrong with that?" He thought of the two of them together, hand in hand or arm in arm. The two of them in public. The two of them admired.

"It depends on how seriously you mean it."

"Maybe it depends on how seriously you want me to mean it." They were moving closer together, almost without willing it. Maybe Lori had forgotten that she didn't need a boyfriend to give her life meaning.

"Very. Very seriously."

"That's good. Because I am serious about you, Lori."

"Ben . . ."

And he touched her, and he knew that he had her. And he knew that he had everything: the glory, the girl, the adoring gaze of the world upon him. Now and forever.

Stromfeld's mocking laughter raked at their ears like talons, shrill, inhuman, the cry of a crow. "Children," he jeered from the monitor screen. "They send children to distract me. Well, I'll send the children back. Look at the counter, little ones."

Cally didn't dare. Her fingers danced over the exposed controls of the door, the steel door that had shut them into the suffocating metal room and was obstinately refusing to open. Her teammates clustered around her, pressed against her. She sensed their increasing panic and desperation. It was like a rising tide primed to drag them down. They did look at the counter.

"Less than a minute!" That was Jennifer.

"What happens then?" asked Lori, sounding like she didn't really want to know.

"Nothing good," answered Jake. "Stromfeld set the trap, and we walked straight into it."

"We are the weakest link," moaned Eddie. "Good-bye."

"Not yet. Not yet." Ben was beside her. "Quicker, Cally, move it! Do your job! Get us out!" He was practically yelling at her, so close that his spittle flecked her cheek. He was going to grab her. Any second now, he was going to grab her and shake her and she couldn't think — there was too much pressure. And in a voice suffused with sarcasm: "You're the expert."

"Lay off her, Ben," yelled Jake. Cally registered that he was defending her. "She's doing her best!"

"Her best? That'll look good on our tombstones. RIP Bond Team — Cally did her best!"

Stromfeld applauded from the screen, his gnarled hands like claws. "Bickering children. You should have stayed in the playground and let your mommies wipe your noses."

"I shouldn't talk noses if I were you." Eddie winced at Stromfeld's hooked and hawkish example. "Must have been the first sign of the slide when Newbolt designed you."

"Shut up . . . I can't . . ." The controls seemed to swim in front of Cally's eyes. She needed a combination. She'd seen systems like this before. She'd been attuned to them. But she couldn't do it. The others were shouting at her and relying on her and she couldn't do it.

She shouldn't be here.

Ben was howling. "Now, Cally, now!"

"Doesn't time fly when you're in a death trap?" Eddie's final quip.

She didn't need to see the counter to know that it had just reached zero. Her teammates raised their voices as one.

The shiny steel floor of the room dropped away. A mile of sky between Bond Team and the ground.

"Farewell, children," said Stromfeld.

"At least the program terminated before we actually hit the ground." Eddie searched for crumbs of comfort. "I wasn't looking forward to going splat."

"Yes, and after all," Lori chimed in, largely for Ben's benefit, "nobody expects a team to beat Stromfeld on the first try. Everybody says that, even Corporal Keene and Senior Tutor Grant." She looked to the others for support, as they were all slumped in various degrees of gloom in the boys' room. Support was not immediately forthcoming."

"Nobody expects. Everybody says," Ben fumed. "We could have been the first, then. Think about that. The first team to conquer Stromfeld at its first attempt. We'd have gone down in the annals of Spy High."

"Instead," Eddie moaned, "we went down the tubes."

"Spilled milk," offered Jake, like Lori, largely for Ben's benefit.

"We can't change what's done so there's no point worrying or dreaming. We just have to learn from it for next time."

"Oh, brilliant, Jake. Is that the wisdom of the Domers or what?" Ben stood and crossed over to Cally. "I've learned something, though, I can tell you. Some people aren't as clever as they think they are."

Cally looked up at Ben. She tried to give him a defiant glare, but her own sense of inadequacy defeated her. "What's that supposed to mean?" she asked, trying not to betray her hurt. She couldn't give Ben the satisfaction.

"Work it out. You're the techno-wizard, Cally, or should that be witch? Or should it be almost-techno-wizard? That door was your responsibility. If you'd been up to the job, if you'd known what you were doing, we'd have been out of there and still in the program. Your responsibility." The accusing finger.

Cally tried to speak, but something in her throat wouldn't allow it. She appealed silently to the others. No one was looking at her.

Except Jake. "Why don't you just leave Cally alone, Ben?" he asked.

Only Jake, Cally thought.

"The truth hurts, doesn't it?" Because he evidently didn't want to.

"Excuse me." She couldn't take it any more. She didn't have to take it anymore, not when she could simply leave the room and all these people she didn't know behind and just keep on walking. "I'm out of here."

Jake snorted and shook his head. "Another fine demonstration of leadership qualities, Stanton."

But Ben clearly didn't care.

IGC Data File DWG 8190 (ref. DWE 7882)

... wider investigation called for as the number of disappearances within
and around the Wildscape area continues to multiply. People are just leaving home and not coming back. ...

The academy's resident holograms were turned off at lights out,
allowing the redoubtable Mrs. Crabtree to go home at the same
time for a well-deserved rest. So nobody, living or computer
generated, was likely to be there in the foyer to notice Cally
leaving, nobody to wave her good-bye (*and good riddance*, Cally
thought darkly).

She still kept herself to the deepest shadows, to the corners
of the academy and the edges of the corridors (pretty much the
story of her life at Deveraux). She still wasn't taking foolish
chances. She'd crept out of her room holding her breath and
without even a bag. Packing a few personal items could have
been interpreted as suspicious, although maybe Lori and Jennifer would have approved of her intention and packed her
things for her. Cally wasn't worried, anyway. Possessions had
never been important to her. Living on the street, how could
they be? And going back there, she didn't need anything. Cally
Cross didn't need anyone.

But it surprised her, standing there in the foyer: the slight
lump in her throat, the prickle at the back of her eyes. Why
couldn't she just go? Why the hesitation?

"I'm afraid the office is closed for the day." She jumped, star-
tled, as Jake emerged from the darkness like a swimmer from
black waters. "Anything I can do?"

"Jake," she said nervously. "What are you doing here?"

"Asking you the same question."

"Oh, me." Cally turned her face to the shadows and hoped they would hide her. "I . . . ah, I couldn't sleep. Thought a walk might . . . I'm going for a walk."

"A long one?" wondered Jake. "All the way back to the city? Trouble is, Cal, no matter how far you walk, you'll never find your way back there. There's no going back."

"What are you talking about?" she asked, with an unconvincing laugh. "I'm only going into the grounds. I'll only be a few minutes."

"If you go through these doors now," Jake predicted, "you'll be leaving for good, and we both know it. I guessed you might try something like this after Ben's rousing little pep talk. Wanted to stop you from making a big mistake."

In the darkness, she was alone with Jake. There no longer seemed any point in protesting. She didn't have the strength. "All right," she admitted. "I'm going. For good, yes. I don't belong here. Nobody wants me here. Nobody'll miss me. I was an idiot to listen to Grant in the first place."

"No, you weren't." Jake spoke the words with such gravity and conviction that Cally thought he must be referring to somebody else. "You do belong here, Cally, just as much as any of us do. You were right to listen to Grant. Where you'd be wrong is to listen to Stanton."

"But what Ben said, Jake. The Stromfeld program — it *was* my fault."

"Partly, maybe, but you're not the only member of Bond Team. There are six of us. We all have to take our share of responsibility, even our great leader."

"Do you think so?" Cally was looking anxiously at Jake now, for reassurance, maybe even for something else.

"I know so." He chuckled wickedly. "And it was almost worth failing this one time, wasn't it, just to see Stanton's face? Looked like he was chewing on a wasp."

"A swarm of wasps." Cally laughed, too. It felt good.

"Don't leave because of him." Jake was serious again. "But don't stay because of him, either, Cally, to prove a point out of spite. Whatever you do, do it because it's what you want. Trust yourself. Believe in yourself."

"But Jake," Cally shook her head, "these people here, they're not like me. Have you seen how many black students there are here? I can count them on my thumbs. And Ben, Lori — they're rich, you can tell, they've had good educations. I can't compete with them."

"Bullshit," Jake rejected. "Defeatist bullshit, Cal, and you know it. What we were before we came here means nothing. Stanton's big house and posh school and stacks of cash don't impress Grant or Keene or Stromfeld, do they? Nobody plays favorites around here. Your experience — living on your wits, surviving on the street — that's more useful now, more relevant to what we're training for than money in the bank and a fancy address."

"You might have a point, Jake." She believed it. She wanted to believe it.

"Besides, not everybody here's like Ben or Lori. I've heard they even let the odd Domer in, and you can't get much lower than that." He grinned ironically.

"Jake," Cally disapproved with mock severity, "now who's spouting defeatist bullshit?"

"Well, maybe the two of us had better stick together, then," Jake suggested. "The outsiders — Bond Team's Social Rejects

Division. Maybe we ought to make sure we're there for each other, good times and bad. Can't let Stanton have it all his own way."

"No," said Cally. "I'd like that, Jake."

Jake nodded. "Still needing a walk?"

Cally smiled. "I don't think so. Suddenly, I think I'll be able to sleep without one."

"Then let me take you back to your room."

"Thanks, Jake," Cally said. "For being here."

"I'll always be here," Jake said.

IGC Data File Priority Access Chal 008

Agent Challis has failed to report in from his assignment at New England Division of Genetech Incorporated. Agent Challis has been directed to contact base three times at half-hourly intervals in accordance with procedure and has not done so. Conclusion: Agent Challis is somehow incapacitated. IGC scanning for information re: possible techno-terrorist attack on New England Division of Genetech Incorporated. . . .

IGC Data File DWG 8199 (ref. DWB 7604/DWF 7900)

. . . not the first Genetech installation to be raided and perhaps unlikely to be the last. Early reports suggest that casualties were minimal, although several security personnel do appear to have vanished during the incident. . . .

IGC Data File Priority Access Chal 009

Agent Challis still unable to be contacted. Body of Agent Challis not found, nor any trace of him. Conclusion: Agent Challis has been abducted by enemies unknown. Prepare form letter to send to parents of Agent Challis re: accident while on Outward Adventure course.

CHAPTER SIX

Present Day

On the night of Bond Team's second failure at the Stromfeld program — the one in which the bickering between Daly and Stanton had reached catastrophic levels — Senior Tutor Elmore Grant received a call from Jonathan Deveraux. He'd been expecting one. That was partly the reason why he'd been sitting at his desk staring at the students' first day photographs and raking over the past. He hadn't had to report Bond Team's disaster to Deveraux himself. The founder knew everything.

"Grant, we need to talk."

"Yes, sir. I'll be right up. Is it Bond Team?"

"Partly, Grant, partly. Also Agent Challis."

Grant winced. As if his present students weren't enough for him to worry about, there was also Will Challis's disappearance. If you went missing in the spy game, chances were you wouldn't be coming back. "Still no sign?"

"No sign," said the voice of Deveraux. "We must, I am afraid, assume the worst. But we need to talk, Grant. I have an idea I would like to put to you. And it may be Bond Team's final chance."

There was going to be trouble. Lori could sense it. Ben was tense and clenched and raging inside, had been since the latest Stromfeld debacle. Grant's criticisms of the team generally and of him in particular had darkened his mood further. Anything less than total success in everything that he did was like an infection to Ben, a disease eating him away. She'd known him long enough to learn that. Maybe that had been part of the attraction, becoming the girlfriend of a boy who was always driving himself, forcing himself to achieve, who was never satisfied with second best. She wanted to fulfill herself, too, in every way. At its best, it was one of Ben's strengths. But at its worst, it was a dangerous weakness. And tonight, it meant trouble.

The atmosphere in the recreation room was already wilder than usual — louder, more excitable. It was like Christmas and New Year had suddenly arrived together and had to be crammed inside an hour. Of course, Lori could understand why the students from the other first-year teams seemed so hysterical. They'd all passed the Stromfeld program. For them, the rest of term would be a formality. Only Bond Team hadn't and Ben, fuming beside Lori with an untasted drink in his hand (had it been arsenic, she suspected, it would have been downed in one gulp), seemed to be interpreting everybody else's celebrations as a personal affront designed to complete his humiliation. It was just as well that the others, particularly Jake, weren't around.

Unfortunately, Simon Macey was. She could see the leader of Solo Team lounging by the refreshments table with several of his teammates. He kept glancing in their direction with a smug, self-satisfied smile. Lori could almost see a thought balloon above his head: *"Should I go over and rub Stanton's failure in his face? Should I?"* She knew that sooner or later, he'd decide on yes, and then Ben would snap. It was probably better that they leave.

"It's a bit noisy in here tonight, isn't it?" she hinted to Ben.

"So go find a quiet corner somewhere if it bothers you."

This was clearly going to be difficult. Lori gently squeezed his shoulder. "Why don't we find a quiet corner big enough for two?" Sounding seductive in a crowd of blaring students was not easy. "You need to relax, Ben. I've got one or two ideas."

Ben flicked her hands away like dandruff. "I'm not in the mood. I'm relaxing here."

"But don't you think —"

"No, I don't. And don't tell me, either." Ben's face contorted in anger. Simon Macey saw it and was delighted. "I've got as much right to sit here as anybody else. They haven't thrown us out of Spy High yet."

And then it all seemed to happen at once, like a film that had been sped up to reach the exciting part. Cally entered with an eager Eddie in tow. Simon Macey made his move. All three bore down on the glowering Ben.

"Look, it's Cally and Eddie," Lori said, waving to them, hoping they'd get there first.

"Terrific," Ben muttered.

"Evening, Stanton." Simon Macey had seized his chance.

Ben glared up at him. "What do you want?"

"I'm worried about you, that's all. I mean, we're all students of Spy High, aren't we? At least for now. I'm just looking out for you."

"You might need to look out for yourself if you're not careful," Ben threatened.

"Simon, maybe it'd be better if . . ." But nobody was listening to Lori. She turned to the newly arrived Cally and Eddie for reinforcement.

"Ah, that's just like you, Stanton, isn't it?" Simon Macey

shook his head in mock sympathy. "Always on the defensive. Always the big 'I am.' Not a team player."

"Hey, Macey." Eddie saw where all this was heading. "Talk to someone who's interested."

Simon Macey ignored Eddie and thrust his sneering face provocatively close to Ben. "Maybe that's why you failed Stromfeld today, Stanton. The rest of us passed, did you know that? We passed. You failed. How does that make you feel?"

"Final warning, Macey," gritted Ben.

"'Cause let me tell you, it makes me feel *good*."

"Don't let him rile you, Ben."

"Macey, were you born a jerk or have you had to work at it?"

Simon Macey put in one last thrust. "I just wanted you to know, Stanton, after you've failed Stromfeld for the third time, and after you've been invited to leave, and after they've removed your memory of all the things you've done at Spy High and all the people you've known, I wanted you to know that I'll still be here, and I'll be remembering you now and again. And I'll be laughing."

"Yeah?" Ben smiled down at the table. "Through broken teeth."

In one lightning movement he threw his drink in Simon Macey's face and sprang onto him, the two of them colliding heavily with an adjacent table, scattering both glasses and students.

Ben pummeled Macey's face, pounding at his nose. Blood sprayed, the color of Ben's anger and frustration. He wanted to see more of it. He would have, too, only Eddie clamped hold of his fist and tried to drag him away as Macey squirmed like a landed fish on the tabletop. Then Lori forced herself between the two combatants. She yelled at Ben to stop, but the words didn't seem to make any sense to him.

"You could have broken my nose!" Macey protested. His teammates helped him to his feet. "I could report you for this, Stanton. You could be expelled by tomorrow. Unprovoked attack on a fellow student."

"Very provoked," Lori corrected.

"If Ben goes down, you'll go down with him, Macey," promised Eddie.

Ben didn't trust himself to say anything. Not with so many others around him, laughing and jeering. He remembered his touchdown. He remembered being hoisted high, a hero. He had to hold on to those memories.

"Yeah, well." Simon Macey mopped his nose. "No need to report it. The way things are going for Bond Team, we'll be seeing the end of you soon enough. I'm counting the days." He gestured to his teammates. "Let's go."

"All right." Eddie ushered the rest of the onlookers away. "Nothing to see here. Feel free to resume your normal lives."

Lori stroked Ben's hair. "Are you okay? Ben, Simon Macey's not worth —"

"Don't touch me." He pushed her from him.

"Ben," cautioned Cally, "Lori's only trying to help."

"I don't need help," Ben shot back. "I don't need anything. Just leave me alone."

He stormed out. Lori started to follow him. "Maybe you should let him go, cool down for a bit," suggested Cally.

Lori smiled faintly. "I can't. He needs me."

"Whatever you say."

Lori hurried after Ben, but he was already out of sight. She shook her head. Brawls in the rec room, conflicts, and confrontations. She only hoped that Jonathan Deveraux wasn't somehow watching all of this and holding it against them.

It was probably just as well, then, that Lori was not privy to a conversation taking place at that very moment, several floors above where she was standing and in a suite of rooms that she had never entered — where very few people were *ever* permitted to set foot.

Senior Tutor Elmore Grant was one of the chosen, although right now he was wishing that he'd been passed over. "Are you sure this is a good idea, sir?"

"Are you questioning my judgment, Grant?" Deveraux's voice was mildly amused.

"No, sir, of course not." Grant ran his hands through his hair. "But a gamble like this, the possible dangers involved, with Bond Team still so volatile and unpredictable . . ."

"Possible danger is something our students have to live with every day of their training, Grant, you know that," Deveraux said. "Because in time, the possible becomes actual, as Challis, Tate, and countless others have discovered. Don't you have faith in your selections? Don't you have faith in Bond Team?"

"Yes, sir, I do, but at this stage —"

"Then we will see. Arrange it, Grant. The moment of truth for Bond team is coming, and it will either make them —" Grant nodded his head in agreement with his superior — "or break them."

*   *   *

If the hologym had been human, it would probably have tried to dissuade Ben from activating it in his present state of mind. "Holoprograms are not to be taken lightly," it almost certainly would have said, "participants need their wits about them. Better come back tomorrow when you're calmer." But even if the hologym had been a living, breathing being, rather than an intricate web of sensors and circuitry, Ben still wouldn't have listened.

He strode into the gym's empty, echoing arena as if he were advancing on an enemy, aggressively pulling on his shock suit, his holohelmet rammed tightly onto his head. "Run ninja program," Ben instructed through the helmet's communicator.

"Voice pattern recognized," the system responded. "Which level of difficulty would you like today, student Stanton?"

"Advanced." He didn't plan on playing.

"Which zone of engagement would you like today, student Stanton?"

"Three." It was the tightest setting, giving him the least room to maneuver and nowhere to hide. Through the electronic eyes of his helmet, Ben saw the circle drawn within which he would fight.

"Which level of electrical current would you like today, student Stanton?"

"Three, again." The maximum. Ben was almost masochistically determined to prove himself. The shock suits worked two ways: On operations, they could be employed as an unexpected weapon to electrocute assailants, but in the hologym, they could be turned against the wearer to increase the stakes in any combat program. Now, every time a holographic fist or foot would strike Ben, he would feel it. His own suit would make sure of that.

But Ben wasn't intending to be hit. "Begin," he commanded. "One ninja."

The figure was behind him, silent, stealthy, robed in black. But Ben's holohelmet included a radar-vision feature. There was no creeping up on him tonight. He pivoted, smashed out with his left leg. The hologram flashed red where he struck. Perfect crunching contact. The ninja fell. Ben imagined it was Simon Macey. "One ninja," he ordered, and a second threatening shape appeared, this time ahead of him to the right. Ben though that this one had more of the stance of Jake Daly. *Excellent. Hello, therapy.*

He should have headed straight to the hologym after their Stromfeld debrief with Grant, Ben reflected. He should have worked off his frustrations in the first place, as he was doing now. This would have denied Simon Macey the tawdry triumph of making him lose his temper in public and stopped Ben from exposing to everyone exactly how much he was smarting at Bond Team's shortcomings and at himself as failed team leader. He should be setting an example.

This kind of example, Ben thought, as a dazzling combination of blows sent the second ninja into scarlet disintegration. *Too easy. The safe, halfhearted kind of challenge that second raters like Eddie or Jake or Simon Macey or the girls would settle for (or anyone, indeed, apart from Benjamin T. Stanton Jr. and maybe Will Challis). He'd been born for better.*

"Two ninjas."

One on each side circled him.

Macey had disturbed him more than he'd cared to admit with his reference to the Amnesia Rule. All of the students knew that that was their fate if they failed. The clandestine nature of

Spy High was paramount; nobody could be allowed to compromise that. So if any student dropped out or could not graduate for any reason, his or her mind would be wiped clean of knowledge of the school and its purpose, and implanted instead with false memories. It was the ultimate nightmare for Ben, who'd always believed that his name was destined to be printed in large type on the pages of history. It was a scary thought: that he himself might be deleted, erased, his ambitions denied him as if they had never been.

Ben swayed, parried the first ninja's blow, chopped down forcefully on his neck, and saw a red welt flare up. Then he whirled and kicked at the second, following up with an expertly executed throw. Both figures dissolved in defeat. And Ben wasn't even out of breath. He felt his confidence returning to him, strengthening him, emboldening him.

"Three ninjas," Ben dared.

He immediately started to regret it. Now not only were there more foes for him to fight, but they seemed to have learned from the fate of their predecessors. The new ninjas contented themselves with circling him, keeping themselves out of the range of his blows. They were moving together, in a pattern, coordinated, awaiting his error. It was as if they were in silent communication with each other.

Ben frowned. Were the holograms supposed to be able to work together? How was that fair?

Then he remembered. Technically, three ninjas or more should only ever be tackled by pairs or teams of students. The good guys work together to beat the bad guys. That was the idea.

Well, here was one good guy who could flatten the villains on his own.

Ben struck suddenly. Red. As his first opponent stumbled, Ben grabbed his holographic sleeves, and bent his weight to throw him. But the ninja recovered, struggled. And a level three electric shock jabbed into him as a second foe struck him from behind.

Ben cried out — in shame more than in pain. He had enough strength to propel the first ninja into the second and enough nimbleness to parry the thrust of the third. Doing so reestablished the balance of the conflict.

But he'd been hurt. He was surrounded, encircled. And his enemies would not fall.

Cally had been sitting in the rec room for over half an hour now since the fight, but Jake still hadn't put in an appearance. She supposed she should have realized that Jake was likely to ditch the party in case Ben was there, bitter and brooding. Well, he'd made a good call. So now she had a choice: either to sit and endure Eddie's apparently inexhaustible supply of moronic one-liners, or to leave him to it and seek Jake elsewhere. In reality, there was no choice at all.

Because she needed him now. She really needed to see him. Since Jake had stopped her from walking out on the school, she'd tried, struggled, and strained to fit in, and, for the most part, she'd succeeded. Her grades were stronger, her computer skills in particular gaining increasing respect, even from Ben on one or two grudging occasions. She was beginning to feel less like an outcast and less like a failure.

And then Stromfeld had to come along and ruin her sense of progress again. Her self-esteem had been obliterated with the bomb. Back to square one.

Back to Jake.

She could tell Eddie was disappointed. He attempted to disguise his feelings with an "Excellent, gives me a chance to share myself around a bit," but it was about as convincing as a pair of dark glasses and a false moustache. She patted him encouragingly on the arm as she left. It wasn't Eddie's fault that he wasn't Jake. He was nice in his own way. Cally even forgave him that ridiculous incident during the SkyBike race.

But it was Jake's reassurance that she needed now, his strength and words of comfort. And, she realized, consciously for the first time, that she also needed something more.

Electricity stabbed into Ben's stomach, twisting like a blade and crackling along his spine like a lightning rod. Ben cried out. Had his eyes been open and not jammed tight in pain, he might have expected to see his shock suit blacken and burn as the ninjas ruthlessly and remorselessly cut him to pieces.

He was flailing now, floundering — all discipline in his defense lost. He was an easy target. He was dead meat. But holograms did not feel pity or mercy, and they could not be stopped with screams.

But he *could* stop them. He could end the torture by uttering two small words into his communicator: End program. Ending the program would end the pain. But it would also signal defeat. And even if nobody else would ever know, Ben would. He'd know he'd failed, and so he resisted, as shock after shock daggered into his body.

Then he was falling. He felt himself toppling into unconsciousness. And the ninjas would continue their assault even then, and he'd be twitching on the floor, sparking like a broken fuse. He had to stop it now, regardless. Ben opened his mouth to fail. . . .

And the ninjas vanished.

"Program terminated. Thank you for playing, student Stanton."

Ben took a deep breath, his body rippling with pain but his mind alive. *What happened?* He hadn't said anything. He hadn't surrendered. But who had?

He felt her arms around him, helping him take off his helmet. Her lips were on his brow, his cheek. Lori had saved him. "Ben, Ben, what did you think you were doing?"

"Lori, I . . ." But he couldn't explain.

"Are you trying to kill yourself? I saw the settings. No one can take on three ninjas in that amount of space."

"I did."

"And survive, I mean. Ben, look at you." Her concern was genuine. "And you know what's the strangest thing? When I saw you fighting, I could only see you, not the holograms. You were the only one who could see them. To me, you weren't battling anyone — only thin air, only yourself. I know you feel bad, Ben, but you've got to let someone in, someone real. Let me help you."

"Help me?"

"It's going to be fine. Everything is going to be all right."

Ben hoped so. He clutched at Lori, and he held her tight, and he hoped so.

But he had his doubts.

Jake liked to be alone when he gazed at the stars. Other people wouldn't understand what the experience meant to him, and he wasn't thinking some sentimental romantic nonsense about the twinkling jewels of the heavens. No, for a Domer — born and bred in a perfectly controlled environment, with horizons pinned by metal arches and the roof of the world a scientifically shaped and measurable glass panel distanced high above your head — it was the vastness, the illimitable hugeness of the naked night sky that impressed, that shocked. There were documented cases, Jake knew, of individuals who had left the domes for a short time and not been able to cope with it, who had to be returned before they went mad. The current medical explanation was that every Domer in the country was a potential agoraphobic. Jake intended to be the exception. Open spaces were, to him, not a source of fear but of hope, not a threat but a promise. The dome had been a prison, and now he was free.

Tonight, though, he hadn't stolen outside solely to relish the emptiness of the night, the chill breezes that, like all temperature and weather variations, were still new and enticing to him. Tonight, Jake needed to be alone to organize his thoughts and to decide what to do, most of all what to do about Ben.

Benjamin T. Stanton Jr. Even his name represented everything that Jake loathed and despised about the world. Every syllable reeked with power and position. The ridiculous "Jr.": The name was itself a valuable legacy that ensured the perpetuation of privilege. The haves and the have-nots. The injustices and unfairnesses of society. Benjamin T. Stanton Jr. symbolized the system that preserved the gulf between the rich and the poor, granting everything possible to those born with wealth while condemning those unlucky enough to have been born into poverty, or in want, or beneath the stifling steel of the domes, to a life shorn of ambition and deprived of dreams.

Little wonder that Jake was finding it difficult to get on with Ben.

Partly (he wished completely), it was Ben's fault. The snide comments. The barely disguised contempt for Jake's background and therefore, by extension, for Jake himself. The breathtaking arrogance. The egotism. The way he treated people, even his teammates, as if they were training not to be spies but servants and their master was going to be Benjamin T. Stanton Jr. Jake knew he wasn't the only one to dislike Ben. There was Cally, at least. How Lori could tolerate him as a boyfriend — allow him to put his pampered and well-manicured hands on her — Jake couldn't understand. But then, he wasn't good with girls himself.

Back to Ben, though. One problem at a time. And the problem was that his animosity toward Ben (and vice versa, to be fair) was now having a seriously detrimental impact on the effectiveness of the team. Ben wasn't the only one to blame. It galled Jake to admit it, but he was contributing, too.

Like today, for example. Stromfeld. The bomb. The disagreement over red wires and blue wires. Jake wished he could convince himself that he'd contradicted Ben entirely and exclusively because he absolutely and assuredly believed Ben to be wrong and himself to be right. Not just because he wanted to rankle the team leader in a moment of tension. Or worse, not just because taking the opposite position for the sake of it was fast becoming a point of principle with him. But he couldn't be that dishonest. He'd delayed Ben from defusing the bomb until it was too late. He'd done it simply to score points off his rival.

And Ben had been right all along.

So how did Jake feel now? Hadn't he demonstrated exactly the same kind of prejudice toward Ben that Ben had so often demonstrated toward him? So how were they any different? How could Jake continue to claim the moral high ground?

He looked up thoughtfully to the stars, but they didn't seem likely to provide an answer. He wondered if anything would.

Then: "Who is it?" He heard her approach before the visual evidence.

"It's all right. It's me." Cally said, smiling, a little too keenly. "I've been looking for you everywhere."

"Yeah?" He didn't really appreciate the intrusion. "Well, I haven't been everywhere."

"No, I can see that. Isn't it a bit cold out here?"

"Not for me." Jake struggled to keep the irritation from his voice. "Did you want something?"

"Just to talk." She paused uncertainly, sensing his coldness. "I blew it again, didn't I? With the Stromfeld program. It was my fault. . . ."

"Cally, not this again." He was finding that he couldn't help himself. He didn't want to snap, not at Cally, but he had his own Stromfeld-related issues to deal with. He wasn't her psychiatrist. "What did I say the last time?"

"I can't remember word for word," Cally said, like a child on the verge of tears, "but there was something about the two of us sticking together. There was something about you always being here."

Ouch. He'd been too short with her. "Sorry. I'm sorry." Jake moved toward Cally repentantly. "I didn't mean to . . ."

"No, it's all right," Cally said, evading him defensively. "Don't worry, Jake. It's my fault. My fault again. Actually believing. Just keeping me happy, weren't you? Foolish of me to think you might actually . . ."

"Might actually what? Cally, wait. If you want to talk . . ."

"No, no, I'll leave. You obviously want to be on your own. It was stupid of me to come looking for you, but don't worry. I won't make the same mistake again."

"But you haven't made . . . I was just distracted, what with today and . . . Cally, don't go."

"Got to." Cally flashed Jake a bitter farewell smile. "But you know something, Jake? You've got more in common with Ben than you think."

Jake winced.

Long after Cally had departed, he mulled over what she'd said. He was still considering it when he finally returned to his room. Oddly, Eddie and Ben were sitting up waiting for him.

"What's this? You two practicing to be my parents now?"

"We've just heard some bad news," said Eddie. "On the grapevine. If you loaned money to Will Challis, don't bet on it being repaid."

"What do you mean?"

"Seems Will's latest mission wasn't a success," said Ben. "He's gone." It was difficult to tell what Ben was feeling. Was that lip curled in commiseration or contempt? "And another thing, Grant wants to see us, all of us, tomorrow morning in his study."

"About?"

"We don't know," said Eddie.

"But it sounds important." Ben's voice was grave. "Whatever it is, I think it could decide the future for all of us."

PART
TWO

CHAPTER SEVEN

"*Camping?*" Eddie worried that he'd suddenly developed a hearing problem. "Camp? Ing? As in tents and rucksacks? Didn't that go out with the ozone layer?"

"We feel," said Grant, "that your central problem at this time is one of trust, of teamwork, and that this short camping trip is one way to address that."

"Of course." Ben stabbed a glare in Eddie's direction. "Whatever you say, Senior Tutor Grant. We know you have our best interests at heart."

Indeed, thought Grant, not that Bond Team's collectively dismayed expressions seemed to acknowledge it. Jennifer, in particular, seemed aghast. He tried to conceal his own reservations. Orders, after all, were orders.

"This is the plan, then," he outlined. "You'll be flown to the most inaccessible region of the Wildscape, dropped off there with gear: supplies, maps, signaling devices, everything you might need . . ."

"Shower, holovision, dancing girls," Eddie mumbled under his breath.

". . . to keep yourselves going for three days, and then you'll be left to fend for yourselves. When the three days are over, we'll come to collect you, and you'll return to your normal studies at Deveraux." Grant regarded Bond Team seriously. "Hopefully with a better, fuller understanding of yourselves and each other. I cannot stress how vital this excursion might be to your success or failure in the final weeks of term. Use the time wisely."

"Yes, sir," said Ben, nudging Lori for an echo.

"But, sir," Jennifer couldn't restrain her indignation any longer, "this isn't what I signed up for. I can't just run off into the woods — it's a waste of my time. I need to stay here and work on my judo, my karate. I can't afford to miss Mr. Korita's lessons. I'm asking for an exemption."

"No exemptions," Grant said firmly. "This is not an option, Jennifer. It's an order. And your outburst — placing your own agenda ahead of the interests of the team — is exactly why you have yet to pass the Stromfeld program."

Jennifer frowned at the floor, ashamed.

"Now, does anybody else have anything to say?"

"When do we leave, sir?" asked Ben, earning points for eagerness.

"As soon as the chopper arrives. We'll talk again when you return."

If, a small but nagging voice was whispering at the back of Grant's mind. *If you return.* He hadn't told them everything; he hadn't been allowed. But Deveraux's scheme was a little more complex than a few days of bonding round the campfire.

Grant thought of Will Challis, apparently vanished from the face of the earth. And not alone, either. A number of Genetech employees were also missing. Then he thought of the search that Deveraux had had the IGC perform for any similar recent disappearances. He thought of the results, the location.

Bond Team was in for a shock.

*   *   *

"So this is the great outdoors!" Eddie exclaimed, flinging his arms wide as if to embrace the panorama of the pine-clad hills that plunged and climbed before him. "Where's the nearest burger joint?"

"I think it's beautiful," Lori said simply. She slipped her hand into Ben's and squeezed. Eddie could be cynical if he liked (and he usually was), but from their vantage point, on the barely wooded plateau where the chopper had left them, Lori was struck by the primitive and untamed wonder of the Wildscape.

"Speak for yourself, Lori," Cally shuddered. She thought of the streets where she'd grown up, thronging with people, perpetually lit, always busy, always loud, the familiar concrete sidewalks of the city beneath her feet. This expanse of green silence and the darkness that would soon come, as absolute as death — this was another world to her. It was mysterious and somehow menacing. "Give me streets and skyscrapers any day."

"Well, I doubt that Jake agrees with you, do you, Daly?" Ben said. "This must be like coming home to you, right?" He pointed upwards. "Without the glass sky, of course."

"This is nothing like the domes," Jake said. He breathed in the sweet air deeply. "Not that I'd expect a city boy like you to know it, Stanton. The domes cover flat land, farmland, land that's been conquered by man. This place, this place is different. It still has its dignity, still has its soul. It's free."

"Yeah, well, I can't imagine anyone paying to come here," Eddie remarked. "You and Lori may be getting all back to nature on us, Jake, but me, I'm in countdown mode. Seventy-one hours and thirty minutes to go until pick up."

"Don't be so negative, Eddie," scolded Lori.

"So what are we going to do, stand here and admire the view for three days?" Jennifer stood sullenly apart from the others, as if to illustrate physically her resentment at having to be there at all.

"No, Jen's right," Ben conceded. "We might as well get some exercise, find a place to camp near a stream or something. Let's go."

"Down there? Into the forest?" Eddie wasn't looking healthy. "But there could be bears down there. Or wolves looking for their next meal."

"Don't worry, Eddie," Jake grinned. "Wild animals are really fussy eaters."

Lori laughed and touched Jake's shoulder. "That was nice, what you said about the land being free. I hadn't thought of it like that."

"You haven't lived in a dome your whole life." To Lori, Jake found that he could say it without bitterness.

"No, I suppose not." She regarded Jake with respectful interest. "What's it like?"

But before Jake could respond, Ben intervened. "Hey, Lori, come on. Jennifer's halfway down the hill already. You want me to carry your pack?"

"I can manage, thanks." She raised her eyebrows to Jake in mock despair. "He has to be the man all the time."

"I've noticed."

They descended. They picked their way among the pines, and the forest swallowed them whole.

"You know, Ben, Jake's not as bad as you sometimes make him out to be." Lori was walking alongside her boyfriend, although her glance sometimes strayed behind her, to where Jake and Cally were walking in the rear. Jennifer and Eddie were racing on ahead as if time itself might match their movements and decide to proceed more quickly.

"Is that right?" Ben sounded skeptical.

"I think he's really interesting. I bet he's got tales to tell about life in the domes."

"Well, why don't you walk with him instead and then you can be interesting together?"

Lori sighed. "Jeez, Ben, don't get so defensive. I just think you need to give Jake a chance. Isn't that why we've been sent here? To get to know each other better?"

Now it was Ben's turn to sigh — and frown. He knew Lori was right. But to actively approach Jake, to welcome his company, foster a friendship — Ben wasn't sure he could do it. Not yet. Maybe not ever. They were too different. But did he want to tell Lori that? "I'll try," he said. And smiled.

Lori kissed him lightly on the cheek. "That's good. Now tell me about the Wildscape — Grant wouldn't really have sent us somewhere dangerous, would he?"

Ben shrugged. "I don't think so. The Wildscape is just a protected area, a bit like the national parks used to be before the Great Contamination. When the government built the domes to preserve our food supplies, they also founded the Wildscape Preservation Area, in what used to be the great forests of the northern states and Canada, or what was left of them, anyway." Ben indicated their surroundings. "Guaranteed no development. Strictly limited and recreational access only. To be left as untouched and unaffected by human beings as possible. A landscape that's wild: the Wildscape. Kind of makes sense, doesn't it?"

"If Spy High ever folds, Ben, there's a future for you in

teaching." Lori laughed. Ben laughed. Underneath the canopy of the ancient pine trees, life was good.

"Sounds like Ben and Lori are having fun, doesn't it?" Cally said, pausing momentarily to adjust her pack.

"Are you all right with that? Let me help you." Truth be told, Jake was feeling more than a little guilty over his treatment of Cally the night before.

"About last night" — he wasn't disguising it very well — "I was the one at fault, Jake, not you. Expecting to be able to dump all of my problems on you like that."

"You should have been able to. That's the point, Cal. That's what friends are for. And we are friends, aren't we? Even given the occasional . . ."

"Falling out?"

"I don't know about 'falling.' Maybe just a little wobble."

Cally smiled. "Of course we're friends." *And one day*, she found herself hoping, *something more*. But she wouldn't push it. She'd bide her time. Her chance with Jake would come.

"Hey, slackers, over here!" Eddie called out, waving to them from some distance ahead. "Have a look at this!"

"Would you believe it?" Jake grinned. "Maybe he's found a burger joint after all."

He hadn't. What Eddie had found was a river, crystal clear and cutting its way over the rocky soil. It seemed shallow but flowing quite fast. It was certainly too broad to jump across.

"It's a river," Eddie announced.

"Nothing gets past you, Eddie, does it?" asked Ben.

Jake knelt on the bank, dipped his cupped hands into the water and drank from them. "Delicious," he approved. "Liquid ice."

Cally and Lori dropped beside him and did the same. Ben

might have followed had it been someone else's idea. Eddie was simply shocked. "What are you doing? That hasn't even been sterilized. How can you possibly . . . ? Fish might have done their business in that. And another thing —"

Bond Team never discovered what the other thing was. The sound of rifle fire put an end to that. They were on their feet instantly, into defensive postures instinctively, all senses alert. Eyes raked the foliage with the sharpness of claws. Muscles tensed and breaths bated.

"It's all right, all right. You can stand easy, kids." Shapes emerged from the undergrowth. Half a dozen men appeared, all carrying rifles, all wearing hardy boots, thick check jackets, and woolen hats. "Dan here got a bit enthusiastic. We didn't mean to scare you."

"Dan here" grinned through a beard the color of a fox and tipped his hat. The hat matched his beard, apart from a clumsily stitched-on label in yellow that read "Born to Hunt."

"Hunters, right?" Ben knew that blood sports were permitted within certain quotas in the Wildscape, but only using traditional weapons. No high-tech heat-seeking laser guns here. Had to give the animals some sort of a chance.

"That's right. Nathan Pardew. Pleased to make your acquaintance." Not that he sounded like it. "Now mebbe you'd like to tell me just what you kids are doin' in these parts."

"About to build a bridge, I think," quipped Eddie.

"We're on a camping trip, Mr. Pardew," replied Ben, "if it's actually any business of yours."

Pardew chuckled humorlessly, his companions following suit. Lori noticed that the hunters were gradually forming a semicircle around them. She moved closer to Ben. "A kid with a loaded

mouth," Pardew observed. "Now listen up — you got a name?"
Ben gave it. "Listen up, Ben and Ben's little friends. What you want
to do is forget all about your little campin' trip. What you want to
do is head about ten miles west to the nearest control post and get
your mommies and daddies to come take you home."

"How dare you?" Jennifer looked as though she might get in
a spot of judo or karate after all, but Cally and Eddie squeezed
one shoulder each until she thought better of it.

"Now why might we want to do that?" Jake asked. "Bear in
mind, we've got just as much right to be here as you have." Ben
felt Jake move alongside him. He felt his presence there, and it
was strong, reassuring. "Besides, I think the locals might be hap-
pier to have us around than certain other people I could men-
tion. At least, we don't plan on killing them."

"Kid's got a lip, Nathan." "Dan here" pointed to Jake with his
rifle. "Want me to get him to button it for you?"

"No need, Dan, no need." Pardew shook his head sadly.
"Mebbe you kids don't keep up with the news — mebbe you're
too busy takin' drugs and playin' VR games on your computers
these days — but we're tryin' to give you some helpful advice
here. These woods ain't safe."

"We're not the ones carrying guns," said Lori.

"But mebbe you'll be the ones needin' 'em. Let me tell you,"
Pardew said, "there's somethin' out here. Somethin' loose in the
Wildscape. Somethin' that ain't beast and ain't human. A crea-
ture. A monster. A thing."

"Why didn't you guys tell us you were members of the Big
Foot Appreciation Society?" Eddie piped in.

"This ain't no joke, boy," Pardew warned, and there was certainly no trace of humor in his expression, "and it ain't no story,

neither. Bodies don't lie, and there've been some. Disappear-ances, too. Some of 'em rich folks on campin' trips just like you."

"Well, we don't plan on disappearing," Jake said.

"My brother," "Dan here" broke in, wielding his rifle for em-phasis, "he's seen it. He's seen it, off in the shadows, runnin' in the darkness."

"And we're lookin' for it," said Pardew, seeming to recall his original purpose. "We're gonna hunt it down, and we're gonna kill it, whatever it is. Ain't that right, boys?" There was a muted chorus of agreement. "But until we do, you kids better do more listenin' and less lippin' like you know better than us. Final warnin'. Ten miles west. Control post. Try 'n get there before nightfall. You don't wanna be out at night in these here woods. Sorry to spoil your day. Let's go, boys."

Pardew turned and without another word led his compan-ions back in the direction from which they'd come. Only "Dan here" paused, tipped his "Born to Hunt" hat a second time, re-peated that his brother had seen it, and then hurried after his fellow hunters. Within seconds, they were out of sight.

"What do you make of that?" Jake asked Ben.

"A bunch of nuts," opined Eddie. "Did you see some of those beards? They'd put the Old Testament prophets to shame. I bet it comes from drinking the water."

"Did you believe what they said, though?" Cally didn't look too certain. "Something loose in the woods. What? Big Foot? Some kind of monster?"

"There are no monsters," Jennifer said with contempt. "Sto-ries to frighten children, that's all. Man is the only monster in the world."

"Jenny's got a point," allowed Lori, "but it still begs the

question: what do we do? Head for the control post? Carry on as if we'd never met these hunters? They could have been just trying to scare us, make fools out of us."

"We could radio Grant," suggested Cally, "call Spy High."

"Absolutely not." Ben was emphatic. "No way. Whatever we decide, we do it on our own. Nobody else. The purpose of this trip is for us to be thrown entirely onto our own resources. What's Grant going to think about us radioing home for advice with the first issue we face? That's not going to help us."

"I agree with Ben," said Jake. For a moment, everybody stared, Ben included. "And if you want my opinion, we carry on regardless. Those guys were jerks, and even if King Kong or the Frankenstein Monster or something else has taken up residence in the near vicinity, we're all secret agents in training, aren't we? We're Bond Team. We can handle them. I say let's set up camp here, and think about getting something to eat."

"I agree with Jake," said Ben.

It seemed that staring was suddenly in fashion.

The hunters were right about one thing, Cally thought, as she shifted closer to the fire and wrapped her blanket more tightly around her shoulders, *she didn't really want to be out at night in "these here woods."* She'd take neon lights and twenty-four-hour stores any night of the week. They'd done well building up a considerable fire — she had to concede that — dragging logs and fallen branches to the center of the clearing that they'd made for the tents, but its glow did not penetrate the darkness completely. Cally felt that the night surrounding her was like a yawning black mouth that could close upon them and devour them at any time.

The others didn't seem to feel the same way, or they were better at hiding it if they did. Ben and Lori were cuddled together on the opposite side of the fire, sharing the same blanket and, evidently, the same pair of lips. Eddie was bemoaning the absence of marshmallows — "how can you have survival rations on a camping trip without marshmallows?" — and seemed intent on toasting his fingers by way of compensation. Jake, not too many sideward shuffles away, was gazing into the flames, lost in his own thoughts. Only Jennifer appeared unhappy, uncomfortable, cross-legged on the very rim of the flickering firelight, half-visible, half-lost to the night. But Cally didn't feel up to approaching her.

She made her choice. Shuffled sideways. Jake didn't appear to notice.

"A penny for them," Cally said, giving him a hint. "Or with inflation, maybe it should be a dollar."

"Oh, hi, Cal." Now that he was aware, he seemed pleased to see her. "Coping?"

"I've been warmer." It was a time for hints. Ben and Lori, she was thinking.

"Yeah? Here, take my blanket."

Maybe she ought to write it down.

"You know," as Lori came up for air, "sitting around the campfire like this — dark night, good friends — reminds me of when I was in the Girl Scouts."

"Yeah," said Eddie, "me, too."

"Hello," Ben scoffed. "Didn't they tell you, Eddie? It's called 'the Girl Scouts' because it's only for girls."

"I know that." Eddie leered. "Why do you think I joined?"

"Idiot!" Ben threw a handful of soil.

"It is like Guide Camps, though." Lori loftily ignored the interruption. "All we're missing now is the singing. Want to give it a try?"

"What? Singing?" Ben didn't sound too keen.

"Sure, singing. We used to have one song called 'Land of the Silver Birch' that was nice."

"Yeah, why not?" Eddie encouraged. "Just hear my singing voice, and any beasties in the neighborhood are gonna be on their way to the control post to beg for a transfer."

"I think we might join them," said Jake.

Lori persisted. "It's really nice and really easy. I could teach you."

"Don't bother." Jennifer's voice crackled like the logs on the fire. "This is all a pile of crap!" Flames writhed in her green eyes, caressed her skin as if they recognized one of their own.

"Hey, Jennifer, watch how you talk to Lori," Ben snapped.

"Or what?" Jennifer jumped to her feet. "You can't tell me what to do — not out here. We shouldn't be out here. This is pointless. We should be . . . learning how to fight, learning how to take control, not . . . sitting around a fire and singing songs. Don't you understand?" She looked for some kind of sympathy in the others' faces. When it wasn't forthcoming, Jennifer swore, turned on her heel, and stalked off into the smothering darkness.

"She definitely needs to chill," said Eddie.

"Ben," said Lori, in a concerned voice, "we can't just let her go off."

"Suppose not." Ben made a reluctant move to stand.

Jake stopped him. "It's all right. I'll go."

"I'll keep your place warm," Cally called after him.

He might need it. Plunging into the darkness was like diving into a lake of freezing black water. Jake shivered despite the thermally treated clothes that he and the others were wearing. His eyes began to adjust to the murky light that was filtering through the ebony poles of the pines. Behind him, the campfire was a smudge on a blackboard. The darkness didn't frighten him, but still he hoped that Jennifer hadn't gone far.

She hadn't. She was a shadow among shadows, but Jake found her pressed against a tree, rubbing her forehead against the bark as if to cause herself pain. He remembered how she'd been in the Stromfeld program, and he felt that he wanted to reach out to her.

"Jennifer? Jen? You want to tell me about it?"

She didn't. Even in the darkness she hid her face from him. "Leave me alone, Jake."

"Can't do it." *Don't want to do it.*

"I didn't ask you to follow me."

"I don't think you get any choice in the matter. We're a team. We have to stick together."

"What, even you and Ben Stanton?" Jennifer laughed, sharp as barbed wire.

"We'll get there." *Maybe.* It was colder. Jake suddenly felt it, like a dark chill was passing through the forest. He thought of death, a shroud. "Now are you going to come back to the fire or are we going to have to stand out here and freeze our unmentionables off?"

"You go," Jennifer said, sounding more petulant than genuinely angry now. "I'm staying."

And he wanted to go. Something crawled down his spine

and coiled in his stomach. He sensed a danger in the darkness. But his voice remained normal. "That's not how it works. If you stay, I stay. Simple as that."

"Why are you bothering, Jake?" At last, Jennifer turned to him. "I don't mean anything to you. You don't know anything about me."

"That doesn't mean I don't want to."

"You don't." Jennifer's voice was thick with bitterness. "Keep your distance, Jake. You won't like what you find."

Off to the right, shadows were scuttling. He was certain that he saw something. The darkness seemed to clot and congeal like blood. Jake seized Jennifer's arm.

"Hey, what do you —?"

"Quiet!" His hiss brooked no contradiction. "There's something here with us."

A rustling, like leaves on a tombstone. A panting, like a slavering beast.

"Jake, what is it?"

It came closer. The darkness, alive, twisted into nightmarish shapes.

"Run for the camp!" Jake yelled. "Now!"

They burst into movement. Not fast enough. Jennifer screamed. Jake cried out.

And the darkness was upon them.

CHAPTER EIGHT

"Did you hear that?" Cally stood up nervously. "Was that Jenny and Jake?" She squinted into the surrounding darkness.

She should have looked up.

"Cally, watch out!" Lori saw it first. She and the boys scrambled to their feet.

With a shriek like shattering glass, a creature swooped from the branches. In the second that she had, Cally trusted to her training. She ducked and rolled, feeling claws rake at her hair, her back, but they gained no purchase. A grotesque remnant of a human face blurred by. The animal was furred, snouted, and pointy-eared like a bat. Cally heard its leathery wings flapping, the sound like mummies applauding. It rose in the air and wheeled around for a second assault.

The others were darting toward her, shouting. Moving targets.

Something hard and scaled rammed into Eddie, thumping him to the ground and bringing blood to his mouth. He struggled, but his attacker was too strong — skin like armor pressing him down, green hands groping for his throat. He could see him now: a hideous hybrid of man and reptile. Eddie heard himself screaming.

And then the night turned on Ben and Lori, too, solidified in the shape of twin apelike creatures that looked like the first of a new breed. They howled and lashed at the youngsters with misshapen and mutated arms.

"Back to back!" yelled Ben. "Defend each other! Think hologym!"

He and Lori did so, immediately narrowing the scope of the creatures' attack. Lori's fists made pounding contact with quivering, greasy flesh. It made her want to cry out, but she didn't want to waste her energy. It looked like she'd need it.

Cally was braced for the second swoop of the bat-thing. So was the handy rock she'd seized from the ground, the rock that she smashed into the creature's flared nostrils and sent blood spewing.

Eddie kicked up with his legs and bucked, the sudden shift in movement throwing the crocodile-man off balance. Eddie rolled over. Hands grabbed him. They were Cally's. "What are you doing down there, Eddie?"

"Trying to hide!"

What next? What further terrors? And where were Jenny and Jake?

They were back to back. Battling, fighting hard, fending off the nightmarish creatures that the forest unleashed with clean, clinical blows. *Don't allow the things to grab you, hold you, drag you down. Keep away from the mouths.*

"Hold firm!" Jake cried. "We stand together or it's over! Aim for their eyes!"

A dreadful wail came from Jennifer. "It hasn't got any eyes!"

Lori felt the muscles in her arms ache. *Weapons. They needed weapons. Sleepshot wristbands, maybe, or at least the kitana swords they'd been practicing with in martial arts.* The ape-creature bayed at her and lunged. Lori deflected its attack. *Improvization: The spy who survived was the spy who adapted to circumstances. These were forest circumstances.*

"Branches!" she shouted to the others. "Use the branches like kitanas!"

And fire, Ben was thinking. *Animals fear fire.* As Lori slashed and stabbed behind him with her newly found weapon, Ben plunged his hands into the fringes of the flames, restraining the urge to cry out in pain, and with smoking and blistered fingers, drew forth a burning branch of his own.

At once, a creature matted with hair leaped at Ben. His reflexes were sharp. So was the branch he wielded. It sank into the ape-creature's chest like a stake. Blood gushed from the creature's mouth, and its twisted form burst into flames as it reared back in the agony of death.

And then there was silence.

The remaining creatures were still, their bodies like the hideous sculptures of a deranged artist.

"What's happening?" Lori gasped to Ben.

"Be ready. Stay ready."

And then the things were gone, retreating into the darkness, into the night.

"Is it over?" Terror and tension shook in Cally's voice. "Please tell me it's over."

"Maybe they got a better offer somewhere else," Eddie said grimly.

"What about Jen and Jake?"

"It's all right. We're here." Jake led a limping Jennifer into the clearing. There was blood on his face. They both looked exhausted. "So you had visitors as well, huh?"

"Are you okay?" Ben managed to say it before wincing with pain.

"Better than you, by the look of things."

"Oh, Ben, your hands! Let me see them." Lori gently took them into her own. "They're badly blistered."

"I'll be fine. Anyway, we've got more important things to worry about — like those creatures and whether they'll be coming back."

"Ben's right," said Jennifer. "We can't afford to drop our guard."

"What if they've just gone for reinforcements or something?" Cally was dismayed. "*Now* can we contact Grant?"

"That might be a bit of a problem," said Eddie.

The others saw what he meant. The camp had been ransacked — their supplies destroyed. Everything that was made out of material had been shredded — tents, bedding, clothes — while everything that was solid had been smashed, including their signaling device. There was no way to get in touch with anyone. They were on their own.

"All right, so at least we know where we stand," said Ben. "Options?"

"The control post," said Lori. "Those hunters said it was ten miles west. Even with no maps, we ought to make that."

"Maybe we should have listened to them in the first place," Eddie muttered. "Looks like they were right after all. If we see then again, first thing I'm going to do is apologize. Chalk one up for the boys in beards."

"What we should have done is irrelevant, Eddie," said Ben, who was stung a little by the implied criticism, even given the circumstances. "It's what we do now that counts."

"Yeah," approved Jake, "and we sure can't make a move for the control post in the dark."

"Agreed."

"So that means we stay here, together, by the fire. We stay alert, we don't go to sleep, and we move off at first light. In the meantime . . . we hope those things don't come back for an encore."

"What *were* they, anyway?" Cally remembered her horror. "They couldn't have been natural. More like several different species spliced together. Hybrids. Mutations or something. Disgusting."

"We'll report all this when we get back to school," Ben said.

"Yeah, well, whatever they were," said Eddie, "I hope I never have to see them again."

Bond Team huddled together by the fire. They sat or knelt as before, but now they faced outward, and now there was no suggestion of singing, only listening and looking. They stared into the darkness, their thoughts teeming with the creatures that had sprung out of it. They watched and they waited, and they longed for dawn to come.

It finally did, grudgingly, reluctantly, as gray as the ashes of the fire. Bond Team creaked stiffly into movement as if they were made of wood, their limbs numb and aching, their breaths curling in the cold. "I guess a cup of hot coffee's out of the question," Eddie grumbled.

"Let me look at your hands, Ben." Lori inspected them and winced. Ben's palms were raw and reddened. "Do they hurt?"

"I don't know," said Ben. "I can't actually feel anything at the moment."

Lori pressed her lips against them. "We really ought to put something on them."

"You're doing a good job by yourself, Lori. Don't worry. I'll live."

"Let's hope we can make that plural," said Jake. "Time to go."

Jennifer had wandered over to the charred corpse of the creature that Ben had burned. She touched the scratches on her cheek and coldly stared down at the blackened body. "We got you," she murmured. "We got you."

"Leave it, Jennifer. Come away." Cally's nose wrinkled in repulsion. "It's hideous."

"I've never killed anything before." It was as if the cold reality of his deed had only now occurred to Ben.

"You did good, Ben," Jennifer said darkly. "It deserves to be dead. To be able to kill your enemies must be a fulfilling experience. She kicked at the creature's lolling head. It snapped at the neck like a petrified twig.

Cally transferred her distaste from the creature to Jennifer.

"Did you hear me?" Jake beat his arms against his sides impatiently. "Time to be somewhere else."

"Amen to that," said Cally.

They made their way as quickly as they could through the forest and as accurately as they could in the direction of west. The leaden, sunless sky did not help. It seemed to press down upon them like the lid of a tomb, to be impaled on the jagged branches of the trees. Unlike yesterday, the group now kept close together, sometimes stumbling into one another as the uneven ground dipped and rose. Nobody complained.

"Keep an eye out," Jake warned. "We don't want any more surprises like last night."

Jennifer suggested they all carry fallen branches to use as weapons if necessary. And by the almost loving way that she handled hers, Cally wasn't sure that Jen wouldn't welcome another attack.

"You know," Lori considered slowly, "I don't know what the rest of you think, but it seems to me a bit of a coincidence that, given the size of the Wildscape as a whole, we should find ourselves sent to exactly the same spot as those creatures."

"Just bad luck, Lori," said Eddie. "Story of my life."

"What are you saying, Lori?" Ben was doubtful. "That Grant deliberately packed us off knowing we'd be ambushed and possibly killed?"

"If he wants to get rid of us," Eddie chimed in again, "I'll take expulsion any time."

"I don't know. I just think it's a bit weird, that's all."

"Lori's got a point," said Jake.

"Oh, Lori's got a point, does she?" Ben didn't like Jake siding with Lori against him. "Okay, Mr. Conspiracy Theorist, how about you — wait!" Ben halted abruptly; his whole form tensed.

"What is it?" Jake's sharp eyes pierced the forest.

"You girls wait here. Jake, Eddie, come with me."

Eddie whined. "Can't maybe Lori go with you, and I'll stay with Cally and Jen?"

"Now."

The boys edged forward, Ben in the lead. Jake saw what he had seen, made a grim guess at what it meant.

Eddie gulped. "Is that . . . a man . . . or something?"

Bond Team had caught up with the hunters.

"Maybe it has escaped your notice, Ben Stanton, but women have had equal rights with men for the past hundred years, so if you think you can —" It was Jennifer's turn to forget the rest of her sentence as the girls drew alongside their teammates.

"Oh, my God," breathed Cally.

"Those creatures must have attacked them the same way they attacked us," Ben said grimly, "only they didn't stop until . . ."

Eddie knelt down and retrieved one of the hunters' rifles. It was broken in two like a toothpick. Most of Nathan Pardew lay close by, his beard caked in blood. Eddie shook his head sadly. "Should have listened to your own advice. Should have listened."

"They're not all here," said Jake. "I count four bodies. There were six hunters. I don't see the one called Dan, the one with the Born to Hunt hat."

"Maybe they got away," Cally suggested hopefully.

"Maybe those things took them away," countered Ben.

"Why would they want to do that?"

"I don't know, and I don't want to know." Jake scanned the surroundings. "But there's nothing we can do here. I vote to press on, like immediately."

"What about these poor men?" Lori asked. "Shouldn't we, I don't know, bury them or something?"

"With what?" Ben challenged. "And in this ground? Our first priority has got to be to reach safety ourselves. Then we can arrange for something to be done about these men. And about these creatures, too."

"Yes, Ben," Lori said dutifully.

"Real bodies, though," Cally murmured, "real dead bodies. Part of me hopes we're cozily tucked up in our cyber-cradles and none of this is actually happening. Any minute now Corporal Keene is going to appear and deactivate the program, and we'll find ourselves back at Spy High, and everything'll be normal.

Part of me hopes that. But most of me knows it isn't true. This is all real." Cally looked at the others. "Death is real."

There was nothing more to say. The teenagers continued in silence and with even greater urgency. How far had they walked since first light? Miles, surely, although it was difficult to tell: The forest was always the same, like a book that had been written. How much farther did they still have to go? The distance to the control post diminished with every step, that was the way to look at it. Every step brought them closer to safety. Any second now, they would glimpse the walls of the control post up ahead, solid and secure through the trees. They'd hear the sound of helicopters, the sounds of civilization. They'd break into a run, shouting out in joy and relief, ignoring the pain of their wounds. Any second now . . .

"I see it! I see it!" Cally cried suddenly. "There it is!"

And there *was* something, certainly. Something solid and secure. Something with walls. But the building ahead of them was not a control post.

"It's a lodge," said Ben.

It was made of good, honest stone — a stark defense against all dangers. Gable rooms with timbered windows jutted from its green-slated roof. It reminded Ben of a hotel where he'd stayed while skiing out West a few years ago. Smoke climbed comfortably from several chimneys.

"What's a lodge doing here?" Eddie wondered. "I'm still looking for the sign with 'Middle of Nowhere' written on it."

"Maybe it got lost on the way to a resort," joked Ben.

"Who cares?" Cally pointed to the chimneys. "Smoke equals fire. Fire equals people. People equals help."

At the door they paused, and not just because, despite the evidence of the smoke, the lodge seemed desolate and deserted. Two great totem poles guarded the entrance, one on either side, both carved out with macabre heads — half-human, half-beast, or half-bird — as if animals from all species of the woods were used to ornament the work, randomly and without order. The heads scaled the poles in a chaos of beaks, trunks, and horns. Eyes and mouths gaped with shock.

They were looking at her, Cally thought. *The heads were looking at her. They wanted her to join them in their endless vigil.* "Are we just gonna stand here or is someone gonna knock?" There was anxiety in her voice.

Ben rang the bell. They heard it echo hollowly in the heart of the house. "Someone must live here. Someone must be in."

Lori squeezed Ben's arm. "What if," she began, "the creatures have got here first, like the wolf in Little Red Riding Hood? What if they're already inside, waiting for us?"

"What if you start acting your age, Lori?" Ben responded.

Too late now, anyway. The door opened.

There was a man before them, peering through thick round glasses and blinking like an inquisitive owl. A tall, angular man, who swung his torso from his hips as though the two halves of his body were only loosely connected. A man whose arms seemed too long and whose fingers seemed even longer, white and waxen like candles. A man whose faded gray suit seemed a hundred years old. A man who stood in the doorway and simply said, "Oh, my."

"Hi," said Eddie. "Sorry to disturb you, but any chance of a hot bath?"

* * *

They sat in what Dr. Averill had called the lodge's main lounge and gratefully sipped the sweet, hot tea that the doctor had provided. He'd promised them food, too — ham, eggs, sausage, and pancakes — just as soon as he'd clarified their story in his mind.

"This is a very unusual occurrence, you understand — visitors," he said. "I live all alone out here. The quiet and the isolation, they help me with my work. I don't normally see people here, least of all anybody apparently pursued by, how did you describe them, Benjamin? Nightmarish creatures?" He displayed his teeth in an attempt at a smile. "Perhaps, dare I say it, the product of several overactive imaginations?"

"I can understand how hard it is to believe, Dr. Averill," Ben admitted as politely as possible, "but it's all true. Just look at us."

"Oh, I am looking, Benjamin," said the doctor, "make no mistake about that."

"And what about the hunters?" broke in Cally. "There are dead men out there. We saw them."

"Of course you did."

"Something's got to be done."

"Something will be done, I can assure you."

"This calendar year?"

"Eddie!" Ben skewered his teammate with an icy glare.

Eddie was undeterred. "I mean, shouldn't we be contacting the authorities now? The sooner the better? I mean, what if those things did follow us here? How good are those totem poles in a fight? You don't seem to . . ." He sought words he couldn't find and suddenly seemed to lose interest.

"Oh, we're perfectly safe here." Dr. Averill addressed his teeth to Eddie. "I promise: In all my years of living in the lodge,

I have never been attacked by such monstrosities as you have described. As for contacting the authorities or anyone else, I'm afraid that might prove a little difficult. I live a life entirely divorced from the outside world, totally devoted to my work. I possess no holovision, no videophone, not even anything as old-fashioned as a radio. We are what you might call . . . cut off."

"What can we do, then?" Ben frowned. He couldn't understand the man's calm, his refusal to accept the gravity of the situation. He felt events slipping out of his control. "What can we do?"

Averill twined his fingers together like ropes. "Well, why don't you drink a little more tea and tell me once more exactly what happened?"

Ben didn't want to drink a little more tea. He'd had more than enough. It was too sweet, too sickly, not like any blend he'd tasted before. And he didn't want to tell Averill what happened again, either. He realized he didn't want to do anything other than sleep. All of the trauma catching up with him, no doubt. Let one of the others take over for a change. He'd done his part. They couldn't expect him to lead the entire time, could they?

But the others, it seemed, were no longer even following what was being said. They lolled listlessly, lethargically in their chairs. Eddie's head was nodding gently like he was about to fall asleep. Jennifer stared drowsily at the ceiling, Cally at the floor. Jake seemed to be endeavoring to catch his attention, but slowly, sluggishly, as though any effort to move was too great. His mouth was trying to form words, but Jake seemed to have lost the gift of language. He might have been pointing at something, although Ben couldn't figure out what. It was a struggle to focus.

Averill had given up on him anyway and was somehow now on the other side of the room where Lori slumped before a huge oil painting on the wall. "Ah, admiring my painting, young lady?" Averill said. "It is beautiful, isn't it?"

The picture showed a centaur standing on its rear hooves and beating its human chest, shouting to the full moon. But this was no cozy creature of myth. The human head and torso were slimy with fluid, like the body of a newborn baby. And in the background, in the shadows, frenzied figures — partly human, partly beast — were dancing wildly.

Like the heads on the totem poles. Like the things in the forest.

"I'm so pleased you like it, my dear," Averill said. "It has always been an inspiration for me, for my work."

Ben's tongue was a lead weight in his mouth. "What is your . . . work, Dr. Averill?"

"Ah, that would be telling." A high-pitched giggle, rather disturbing. "You'll find out soon enough."

Ben's eyes rolled back toward Jake, to where he seemed to be pointing. . . .

The table, where the tea was. The table, where the tea had been when they first entered the room. The table that had already been set with six cups, waiting.

Six cups. One for each of them.

Fear gripped the remains of Ben's conscious mind.

Jake, miming hopeless words. Ben knew what he was saying now, knew what he meant. *The tea. It was in the tea.*

"Drugged . . ."

Ben lurched forward. *Had to get away. Escape.* The others were too far gone. It was down to him. He teetered on his feet as the room swayed around him.

"Don't fight it, Benjamin. It's too late, my boy." The high-pitched giggling again. Averill was at his side, inspecting him. "Oh, you're strong, lots of willpower. You'll make a fine subject."

Ben trying to strike him, tottered off balance. Averill was behind him anyway. And in front, coaxing him playfully toward the doorway that was wide like the laugh of a clown. The floor tipped Ben toward it, through it. Averill's white hands applauded.

"Not far now," his voice boomed in Ben's ears. "Just the hall. Can you make it through the hall?"

It was endlessly long, narrow, and didn't seem to have a floor. Ben clutched at some coats that were there to stop himself from falling. It didn't work. He was on the floor. Averill hovered above him, a disembodied head. In Ben's grasp, a hunter's jacket, a hunter's woolen hat. Born to Hunt. Was that whimpering coming from him?

"My earlier visitor's," Averill was saying. "It's been a very exciting day. Now, do you still want to leave?" Ben's body was flesh and bone and did not obey him. "No? Then I think you'd better stay."

Dr. Averill's high-pitched giggle chased Ben into oblivion.

CHAPTER NINE

In her dream, she was in darkness. But she was not alone. Some-one (or some*thing*) else was in there with her, circling her, clos-ing in, and any moment now, the someone (or something) else would stretch out its hand and touch her. And she would scream, but it would do her no good.

Cally fled through the darkness, looking for light. It was there, up ahead of her, a single star like a beacon of hope in overwhelming night. She raced toward it, praying that she could reach it. Because now she realized who was reaching for her, who was almost upon her. Stromfeld. Wanting to keep her here, in darkness, in failure. Stromfeld poised to claim her.

Cally seized the light.

And awoke.

In a room like a hotel room, but she was not a guest. She was lying on the bed, unbound.

Her mind slowly cleared. Her memory returned.

So Averill didn't think she was a danger, didn't believe she could escape? Maybe he'd been privy to her Stromfeld ratings. Or maybe he was simply underestimating her. Cally smiled purposefully: *To be underestimated was to be given an advantage.* The good doctor didn't know he was dealing with students from Spy High. And Cally was one of them. She deserved to be, despite Stromfeld. Now she had the chance to prove it.

She swung her legs from the bed and stood up. She felt strong, balanced, prepared. There must have been a drug in the tea, but at least its effects seemed to have been only temporary.

They'd fallen into Averill's trap unwittingly enough; they'd behaved like novices, perhaps, but Grant had warned them that they could expect to be drugged at some point in their careers, knocked out, captured, and threatened with death from every direction. It was all a routine, part of a secret agent's life, Grant had warned them.

As was escaping, breaking free, and turning the tables on the bad guy. Well, Cally had fulfilled part one of their tutor's expectations. She hoped she was up to part two.

She went over to the window. It provided a deceptively peaceful view of the forest from the upper floor of the lodge. Option one: Smash the window, drop to the ground without fracturing a limb, and run to the control post for help. Not viable on several counts, Cally reasoned. The glass was reinforced, and every stick of furniture that might have doubled as a weapon was secured to the floor. Besides, she ought to locate the others first, and the forest was likely to be crawling with Averill's creatures.

Yes, Cally sensed the truth. Averill's creatures. Somehow there was a connection. In math, two plus two always equaled four. In the spy game, mad doctor plus mutant monsters always equaled dastardly scheme to rule the world. And just as in a Stromfeld program, the time in which to stop it was running out.

Cally darted to the door. Option two: Get out this way, locate the others, find Dr. Averill, and ruin his day. There were no other options. The door was locked, of course, but that didn't matter. Maybe they hadn't worn their shock suits on this little adventure or brought their sleepshot wristbands, but Cally hadn't come entirely unprepared. She was wearing a nitronail.

She did it the way they'd been taught, peeling the transparent sliver of explosive from her fingernail, pressing it firmly against the offending surface — the stubborn handle of the door — and stepping back. Then she counted down from five.

At zero, the nitronail detonated with a muffled boom. The barrier was breached.

It was just like being back at school.

Only here, the danger was real, Cally cautioned herself as she edged out onto what seemed to be a deserted landing. There were more rooms with closed doors to the left and the right, minor corridors branching off from the main landing, and a central staircase farther away and leading down. No immediate threat, it seemed. She could concentrate on finding the others. Solo heroics might be something Ben would go for, but Cally felt that she'd prefer some company right now. She crept stealthily along the landing, accessing in her mind the infiltration techniques that Keene had been teaching them. She came to a minor corridor.

Hands grabbed her and yanked her sideways.

"It's all right, Jake," hissed Eddie. "It's only Cally."

"What's with the 'only'?" Cally returned, though she was glad when Jake's grasp became more of an embrace.

"Nothing," Jake said. "That's just Eddie-speak for 'we're really pleased to see you.' Which we are."

"How'd you get out of your room, Cal?" Eddie wanted to know. "Or do I need to ask?" He wiggled a finger. "Am I hitting the nail on the head?"

"I wish someone would hit you on the head," muttered Jake.

"And our first capture, too, the first time I've ever been

properly drugged." Eddie seemed almost lyrical. "A bit like your first kiss, really. I wonder if we'll get a certificate for it when we get back to Spy High."

"At the moment, that's still an if, Eddie," reminded Jake. "So shut up and concentrate. We still have to find the others."

"So let's start checking rooms," said Cally.

They did. It didn't take long. Apart from those that had contained the three of them, every other room was unlocked and entirely empty of any human occupant.

"Maybe he let them go," suggested Eddie weakly. "Who'd want Ben around, for a start?"

"Don't be stupid." Jake frowned. "Whatever Averill wants us for, he wants all of us."

"So where are they, then?" Cally worried. "What's happened to the others?"

Whenever Lori would wake up, her first instinctive movement was to pass her hand over her face. She didn't know why, maybe to check if it was still there, still her own. So when she tried that now and found that she couldn't move, that was when she knew she was in trouble.

"Welcome, my dear." Dr. Averill was standing over her, his pale fingers coiling together like worms. "Welcome back to wakefulness, all of you."

Lori was bound; she could see that now. She was laid out on a bare metal table with leather straps restraining her arms, legs, midriff, and neck — like a very reluctant patient in a very unsettling operating room. Around her, the room seemed as uncomfortably metallic as the table, gray and soulless. Averill had no doubt chosen the decor himself. She craned her eyes left and right: Ben and Jennifer on either side of her, also stirring. All three struggled against the straps.

"Averill, wait till I . . ." Ben's threat was rather diluted by his helplessness. He jerked uselessly at his bonds. Events were not developing to his liking at all. Didn't Averill realize that he was the leader of Bond Team? His role was to charge in at the last minute and rescue his incarcerated teammates, not to thrash about at the mercy of a madman like a turkey dressed up for Christmas dinner.

"I'm afraid you can't escape," Averill said almost mournfully. "It is a waste of your strength to try, and you may need that later." Jennifer joined Ben in listing in explicit detail and at high volume the things that she would do to Averill if he did not release them at once. The doctor seemed offended. "Such language," he chided, "and from so demure a young lady, too. The manners of young people these days."

At least Jennifer and Lori both seemed unharmed, Ben thought. *They all were, and while that was the case, they had a chance. Be patient. Be alert. Wait for the inevitable mistake. But where were the others?*

"I apologize for the straps," said Averill magnanimously, "but I so wanted a little chat before we got down to business, and I didn't think you'd want to stay if you were not — how can one put it? — encouraged to do so."

"Who are you?" Lori demanded, as aggressively as she could manage. "What do you want with us?"

A high-pitched giggle. "Ah, all in good time," Averill said. "And both will be worth waiting for."

Frustrated, Lori stared down at herself. She suddenly realized that she was no longer wearing her own clothes but was clad in a single garment: a plain, black leotard. Jennifer and Ben were similarly attired, as if they were all about to head off to the gym. Somehow, though, it made her feel all the more helpless, all the more vulnerable. *And what about Cally, Eddie, and Jake? Why weren't they here, too? Had Averill already done something to them?* Tears stung her eyes at the prospect.

Averill leaned over her sorrowfully, wriggled a wormlike finger into the corner of Lori's eye, gently, though, almost lovingly. He licked from its tip the moisture of her tear. "Try not to upset yourself, my dear girl," he advised. "It will not help. And if you are concerned that your feminine modesty may have been violated, have no fear. It was not I who dressed you in something more appropriate for the occasion — I would never conceive of taking such a liberty — but my obedient assistants here."

They shuffled into Lori's vision, chittering mindlessly. They were like ants, evolved beyond a million years to the size of men, chitinous black bodies glistening, thin limbs fondling the air. But in their mouths, human teeth, a human tongue. Between the sections of their bodies were threads of pink, like ancient scars.

Lori fought against giving Averill the satisfaction of a scream, although her face expressed her loathing.

Averill was oblivious. He stroked the hard shell of the ant-creatures as a father strokes the hair of his firstborn. "Beautiful, aren't they?" he admired. "One of my greatest achievements. Designed to work unquestioningly, unceasingly, as the ant in the field does, from the first moment of life until the last. A new race blindly and unthinkingly subservient to its creator." The doctor sighed in self-admiration. "My children."

"Your what?" Jennifer blurted.

"You're sick!" Ben added.

"Genius is always mocked," Averill declared proudly. "The

prophet is never recognized in his own country. Which is why I have kept my true identity from you until now."

"Why, what is it, *Averill?*" Ben jeered. "I've got one or two names I think would suit you."

"Oh, Averill *is* my first name," the doctor admitted, "but my last name is one you may have heard before. I had a notable ancestor, you understand. He was called Victor. Victor Frankenstein. And I am his heir."

They'd made their way to the ground floor again by the book, each in turn slinking ahead, keeping to the shadows, staying to the edges of the walls, seeking cover, keeping low, gesturing with fierce jabs for the others to move up when it was safe to do so. They were now venturing into previously unseen areas of the lodge and Jake, who, in Ben's absence, had seemed naturally to assume the mantle of leader, indicated that they should discuss their next move.

"Maybe we should split up," he whispered. "Cover more ground that way."

"Safety in numbers," Cally whispered back. "At least until we've got a better idea of what we're up against."

"Cue the better idea," gulped Eddie.

They heard voices — male, and more than one — coming their way.

They were in a lounge similar to that in which they'd been drugged. There was a grate for a log fire, although none was burning at present. Large and luxurious chairs were grouped around the fireplace, however, as if they expected additional warmth from that source very soon. Jake, Cally, and Eddie ducked behind the chairs, making themselves small and still.

The voices entered the room.

"Well, at least it's done." Voice Number One, Jake registered, like a contestant in a game show. That was how they'd been taught. If you were hiding and couldn't make out the number of your enemies, count and record their voices, visualize them by their tone, place them in the room by their volume. Make their speech work for you.

"Yeah, well, next time he can get someone else to do it." Voice Number Two, and not happy. "I didn't sign up to dispose of dead bodies."

"You signed up to do whatever Frankenstein tells you to do." Voice Three, a loyalist, but who had he said? Frankenstein? Jake caught Cally's eye across the room. He wondered if his own expression was just as shocked. "And if I were you, I wouldn't complain too loudly. The good doctor's not a big fan of dissent." *The good doctor? Averill? Averill was Frankenstein?*

"What's he gonna do?" Voice Two was not convinced. "Turn me into one of those things, one of his *children*?" There was a pause. Something seemed to have occurred to Voice Two. "Well, at least it's done."

"Didn't take too long, either, did it?" said Voice One, who seemed inclined to look on the bright side. "The genefreaks didn't leave too much to clear up. Me, I reckon they got a better deal than their friends, anyway. You get torn to pieces, it's gonna hurt, yeah, but it's not gonna take long. I'd sooner take that than have the gas on me and get twisted into God knows what."

"Got a point." Voice Three again. "Those kids don't know what's coming."

Jake stiffened. *Neither do you three suckers,* he vowed.

"Where are they, anyway?" Voice Two, and wouldn't he like

to know? Jake was ready for action. He looked toward Cally, who seemed to be counseling caution.

"The three upstairs are probably still bye-byes," chuckled Voice Three coldly. "Guess we might hear them bleating for help any time now. Frankenstein's already taken the blond boy and two of the girls to the factory. Said they looked like the most promising subjects. Wants to work on them first."

That was enough. Jake could scarcely restrain himself now.

"Two of the girls?" Voice Two. "Hope he's left that Chinese-looking one. Fancied doing a bit of work on her myself." Cruel laughter, but laughter always meant relaxation, a dropped guard. Jake tensed. "Wouldn't mind a bit of sweet and sour with her."

Jake sprang.

He didn't care about spycraft now, or watching and waiting, or what the others might say — be it Grant or anyone else. He only cared about Jennifer — and Lori and Ben. He only cared about breaking Voice Two's teeth.

Jake slammed into action, barely registering that Cally and Eddie were following his lead, hardly noticing the pale gray uniforms on Frankenstein's men, or that they'd each been carrying laser rifles, which two of them had fortunately put down on a table. That made the man with the weapon his first priority. A kick sent it spinning from his hand. Jake surged forward, aiming to make the most of the element of surprise. Cally and Eddie were following suit. Cally went low, barreling into her opponent's legs, bringing him down like a felled tree. Eddie went high, vaulting a chair and driving both feet into the third man's chin so hard that his head nearly left his shoulders.

But Jake's opponent was rallying, resisting. He needed to try something different. Jake made a feint, lashed his leg behind the man's calves and, at the same time, rammed his chest with his forearm. The man crashed backward as planned. But Jake did not congratulate himself. Rather the opposite.

The man had fallen alongside his gun, and now he was scrambling to his feet, laser rifle in hand. Now he was pointing it squarely at Jake's chest.

And now, Jake could do nothing about it.

"You must be even madder than you look," scorned Ben, "and that's saying something. Frankenstein? That's impossible. Frankenstein was just a character in a book."

Dr. Averill Frankenstein shook his head in knowing amusement. "Sometimes," he said, "the truth is so shattering, so unacceptable to society as a whole, that it can only be told in the form of fiction. But Mary Shelley knew what she was relating was not a story, but an authentic account of the greatest scientific experiment ever attempted: The restoration of life to the dead."

"So the guy with the square head and the bolts through his neck is somewhere around here, is he?"

The trademark high-pitched giggle. Frankenstein seemed unmoved by Ben's jibes. "Oh, my own research has taken a different direction to that of my revered ancestor," he said. "The mark of genius is originality, and simply to emulate him would be of little consequence to me. Besides, all of that lurking in graveyards, the stitching together of secondhand bodies . . ." Frankenstein dismissed the prospect with a flutter of his elongated fingers. "No, that was never me. Instead, I thought to benefit mankind in a new way."

"Benefit?" Ben wondered if he hadn't misheard. "With these

things, these monsters? You got a different dictionary than the rest of us, Frankenstein? You know what 'benefit' means?"

Frankenstein nodded tolerantly. "You are being too harsh on my children, young man. They are not monsters, but mutations, genetic mutations. Thanks to my innate genius and a few spare parts that my children liberated from various other installations, I have succeeded in mastering the secrets of DNA itself. All of life is mine to play with. Admittedly, the genetic mutation process is not quite perfected yet, but you can't make an omelette without breaking some eggs, now can you? And the progress I have made already, the boons I can bring to man. My warrior children, some of whom you encountered last night, the savagery of beast coupled with the cruelty of humankind, what an army they would make in times of war. And my insect children here, tireless laborers to toil to man's advantage. And these are just the beginning."

"Can we make it the end?" Ben said. "I don't think I can stand any more."

"It's disgusting," added Jennifer.

"And what about you, my dear?" Frankenstein asked Lori. "Do you share your closedminded companions' revulsion at my work?"

"I was going to say you'd created a breed of monsters, Frankenstein," said Lori coldly, "but the only real monster I can see here is you."

"Well, perhaps you'll change your minds if I show you a little work in progress. We have time." The doctor consulted his watch. "A little time." He addressed his ant-children: "Set them free."

The mutants fumbled at the tables. The leather straps holding the teenagers slithered away, allowing them to stand on unsteady feet. Frankenstein's creatures closed in around them, outnumbering them two to one and blocking off any possible escape route.

"Free to an extent, you understand." Frankenstein rubbed his yeasty hands together.

"Where are our friends?" Lori wanted to know.

"Oh, you mustn't concern yourself with them. Your friends will not be joining us."

"What do you mean?" Lori exchanged a frightened glance with Jennifer and Ben. *What if the others were dead, after all?* Suddenly, it seemed obvious to her that they were gone. She felt herself swaying, the room reeling. Repulsive insect bodies hemmed her in. She could endure no more. To collapse back into unconsciousness would be a blessing, to submit to the darkness and never to wake. Strong hands steadied her. Jennifer and Ben both had a steely determination in their eyes. Of course, she could not give up. Of course, she had to endure. She was a student at Spy High, and this was what she had trained for.

"We're still in the lodge, you understand," informed Frankenstein, "but these are my laboratories and experimentation chambers, where I give birth to my children. Now, please," indicated Frankenstein. "Follow me."

"What is this, the grand tour? I hope there's a souvenir shop." Ben made a secret fist for Lori and Jennifer to see. They'd play along with the doctor for now, but their opportunity would come. It had to.

Frankenstein led the way into a dark corridor. Strip-lighting under the floor guided their feet but on either side they could see nothing. Ben wondered whether this might not be their best chance to make a break for it, but the mutant ants surrounding himself, Lori, and Jennifer were too near and too many.

They passed slowly shifting shadows. Sensed the shufflings of unseen life. Heard the wary growls, the despairing moans, the rattling of bars.

What fresh horror was here?

Lori didn't think she wanted to know. She didn't think she wanted to see.

But Frankenstein's eyes were glittering in the dark. "This is where we find the subject observation tanks," he said, and his eyes glinted with pride. "Until the mutation is fully completed and stabilized, I keep my children here. It's like a nursery, if you will. Perhaps you'd like a peek."

No, not at all, anything but a peek, Lori thought. Then she felt a human hand clasp hers. It was Ben.

"Lights up," Frankenstein commanded.

And they saw.

He was going to die. Right now. There wasn't even going to be time for Jake's life to flash before his eyes, and it wasn't as if he'd lived very long.

Frankenstein's goon was squeezing the trigger. He was smiling. Then he was puzzled, his eyes rolling. Then he was sinking with a groan to the floor.

Cally stood behind him, the butt of a laser rifle in her hands.

Maybe Jake wasn't going to die, after all. At least, not yet. "Thanks," he said.

"No problem."

Jake thought he maybe ought to say more, something about

how he was really glad now that Cally had opted to stay, but anything he said in that direction might be misconstrued. It was easier to turn his attention to the only one of Frankenstein's men who was still clinging to consciousness, even with Eddie perched on his chest.

"Where are our friends?" He hoped his tone was suitably not-to-be-messed-with. He retrieved a laser rifle from the floor for emphasis.

"You're too late." Voice Two's voice was recognizable enough, even with blood bubbling at his lips instead of spittle. "You can't save them now."

"I didn't ask for an opinion, scumbag. I asked where our friends were." Jake prodded the man's forehead with the barrel of the rifle. "And unless you want some added ventilation where your brains should be, I'd be quick with an answer."

"You wouldn't kill a man in cold blood," Voice Two gambled. "You're just a kid."

"Yeah?" In a single movement, Jake raised the rifle and fired it at the nearest chair. The laser sliced right through it. He pointed the muzzle back to the man's now perspiring forehead. "Then I'm not gonna get prosecuted, am I?"

"Jake . . ." Cally cautioned.

"Now, I'm going to ask you once more, politely." Jake didn't seem to have heard her. "Where. Are. Our. Friends?"

Eddie glanced up at Jake's eyes. They were full of fury. He was glad Jake was on his side because it was suddenly, startlingly clear that he meant what he said. If necessary, Jake would fire point blank into the man's skull.

Voice Two had evidently reached the same conclusion. "Frankenstein has taken them to the factory. His lab."

"Where?"

"Through there." He tried to gesture with his eyes. "Through the wall."

Cally moved quickly to the room's far wall. Paintings hung from it. Furniture stood against it. It seemed solid enough. Until Cally's arm sank into it as into a ghost. "A hologram."

"Wonder if he uses the same supplier as Deveraux?" Eddie asked.

Cally's head thrust through the wall. "He's right. This is the way."

"All right. Why?" Jake wasn't quite finished with the interrogation. "Why has Frankenstein taken them to his lab?"

"Mutation, of course," laughed Voice Two. "Where do you think those creatures outside come from? If you ever find your friends again, you won't recognize them."

"No? Well your own mother won't recognize you, either." Jake's trigger finger twitched.

"Wait!" Cally steadied him. "Tell us how we can contact the outside world."

"You can't. The only communications are in the factory. Ask Frankenstein if you can make a call. I bet he'll only be too happy to help."

"What about . . . ?" Cally's mind was racing. Like Jake, she wanted to go after the others immediately, to save the day, but what if they failed, like in the Stromfeld program? What if they weren't good enough? They had to have a contingency plan. Spy High and the authorities had to know about this madman and his insane experiments. "What about transport? How do you get about?"

"We've got SkyBikes, girl. Why? Doing a runner, after all?"

"Maybe we'll tell you when you wake up."

Cally nodded to Jake. Flipping the rifle over, he brought the butt down on the man's head. Eddie no longer needed to squat on his chest. He stood up and grabbed the last laser rifle.

"Would you really have done it, Jake?" Cally asked, unsure that she wanted to know. "If he hadn't talked, would you really just have shot him?"

Jake smiled thinly. "Would you?"

"Hey, let's leave the moral dilemmas for later, shall we?" Eddie was eager to get going. "The others need us now."

"No, Eddie," said Jake. "That's where you're wrong."

"Reptiles," Frankenstein explained. "All we have left of the dinosaurs. Armored. Cold-blooded. So many useful applications, from shock troops in battle to a workforce in inhospitable terrain. My program is coming on quite nicely, as you can see."

Languishing in the nearest observation tank was a man whose body seemed green like mold, but whose skin seemed to be hardening, crusting, whose hands and feet were already spiked with claws, woven with webbing, and whose head was reshaping and reforming. It appeared that the mutation was still at work within him. He peeled back his lips to expose rows of alligator teeth. A lost and lonely wail rose in his throat.

"Crocodile tears," ventured Dr. Frankenstein.

But in the next cage, more horrible yet, was someone whom Bond Team recognized, someone they knew: the hunter, Dan, no longer swaggering, no longer brave, his beard flaking off like dead skin.

"Now here is a problem," admitted the doctor, "and one that I hope you might be able to help me with. Serpent and human.

The DNA simply will not combine as I would like. It's the limbs, you see. Mutants without limbs are just not a salable commodity, whatever services one might wish them to perform. And as you can see, even I have so far been unable to develop a strain of my gene gas that can provide the general form of a snake while retaining at least a majority of the humanlike limbs."

They did see. They saw that serpent scales had crept up Dan's body like a dark disease and continued to spread to his neck, to his scalp. They saw his arms stitched uselessly to his sides. What remained of his legs squirmed like a tail.

"It's so frustrating, I'm sure you can understand," sighed Frankenstein, "and I'm so close in every other respect. Ah, well, between serpent and man there has always been enmity, has there not? Since the Garden of Eden. But we creators, we never give up. Now follow me. One more area for you to see."

Frankenstein led the shaken teenagers to the end of the corridor, past more subject observation tanks. It was not tempting to look their way. The corridor opened out on a circular laboratory and control room. In many ways, its computers and screens reminded the three of the core from the Stromfeld program, although the centerpiece here was a great glass chamber that was attached to so many wires and tubes that it might have been on life support. Lori wondered what its purpose might be. Disturbingly, it was large enough for several people to fit inside. A handful of technicians, Frankenstein's assistants — human at least — tended to the chamber, as if preparing it for something.

"The gene chamber itself," Frankenstein announced, his waxen fingers stroking it tenderly. "Like a wondrous womb, granting life to the children of Frankenstein."

"How did this place," Lori struggled for the term, *"this mad-house,* ever get started?"

"Oh, you'd be surprised, my dear," said Frankenstein, "about exactly who has been prepared to finance such adventurous and philanthropic work as my own, particularly since the advent of those interferingly fussy Schneider Protocols. Even governments, you know, are quick to see the military and domestic benefits of my children." Frankenstein's expression momentarily darkened. "Unfortunately, I have to admit, support from those sources has not been quite so forthcoming of late. A few infantile qualms about how I procure my subjects. As if I had not already suggested emptying their prisons for them and fitting criminals for a useful social purpose for once in their misbegotten lives."

"You're all heart, Frankenstein," snorted Ben.

The doctor shrugged. "But greatness is not to be thwarted by men with small minds. You'll be pleased to know, I have been approached by another organization — a type which appreciates the kind of future that my work can bring about for man, a type unrestricted by fear or scruple."

"Techno-terrorists," said Lori.

"Free thinkers," said Frankenstein. He looked again at his watch. "But you'll be able to judge for yourself, won't you? I'm expecting a call from CHAOS any moment now. They're keen for me to work with them, you see. They have in mind many applications for my children, but before they will commit themselves financially, they'd like a live demonstration."

"A demonstration?" Ben felt the words freeze in his throat. "Of what?"

"The gene chamber is primed, Dr. Frankenstein," informed an assistant.

"Thank you, Davis." Frankenstein's trademark high-pitched giggle made Ben's blood curdle. "They want to see how my gene gas works, of course. They want to witness a transformation. And to show good faith, I intend to give them more than one."

"What do you mean?"

"Oh, haven't you guessed yet?" Frankenstein seemed almost disappointed. "Why do you think I've brought you all here? You're the demonstration."

CHAPTER TEN

Eddie powered up the SkyBike and accelerated toward the forest. The lodge grew small behind him before disappearing from view entirely. It was not a place he was looking forward to seeing again.

He supposed Jake was right. Somebody needed to contact Spy High, let Deveraux and Grant know what was going on deep in the heart of the Wildscape. Somebody needed to fetch the cavalry, SkyBike style. And true, he, Eddie, was arguably the most skillful rider in the whole of Bond Team, although Cally wasn't far behind. Eddie couldn't help wondering whether there wasn't something more than an innate faith in his abilities that had led Jake to nominate him for the reinforcements run, something to do with wanting to keep a prettier face around for a partner. The way Cally looked at Jake sometimes, if there wasn't something going on there already, he could tell she wouldn't mind if there was. Which left poor old Eddie Nelligan out in the cold again, an irrelevance. Just like now.

He focused on the navigator between the handlebars of his SkyBike. It was like a radar system, showing where he was in relation to his immediate environment. He'd already keyed in his desired destination: the control post. The bike would take him there automatically. He'd call Spy High. They'd call the army. Situation over. Theoretically, all Eddie had to do was sit back and enjoy the ride.

Theoretically.

A cluster of red lights flashed warningly from the navigator. Eddie had company, closing in fast. He doubted it was friendly.

He glanced behind, glimpsed them in the splashes of green light, weaving between the trees on both his flanks. Franken-stein's men, numbering at least four. On weapons-grade Sky-Bikes. A laser bolt pulsed from the pursuing pack and incinerated a bush that was unsettlingly close by.

Eddie gritted his teeth and hung on. Seemed he had a bit of work to do after all.

"Which way now?"

Jake was aware of Cally's inquiring and expectant gaze. The corridor they'd been following was now branching in two direc-tions. Left or right. Red wire, blue wire. On such simple alter-natives did lives depend, and not just anyone's life this time, but the lives of his teammates. *Maybe it would have been better for Stanton to be here and for me to have been taken by Frankenstein instead,* Jake pon-dered. *At least Ben never seemed to have trouble with decisions.*

"Jake?" Cally was urgent. "Which way?"

"Left," said Jake.

"Any particular reason?"

"None at all."

The corridor continued the trend already established since Cally and Jake had entered Frankenstein's laboratory areas. It slanted subtly but certainly downward.

"We must be underground by now," Jake observed. "Remind you of Spy High — the truth concealed?"

"Spy High exists to help people," said Cally, "to help the world, if necessary. This place, if Frankenstein's responsible for those creatures that attacked us —"

"No doubt about it."

"— then this place is an outrage." Cally gripped her laser rifle more tightly. "And it's up to us to do something about it."

Snarls and growls from up ahead brought them up short. Human voices, too: "Keep moving, you freaks. Dumb mutants. Don't know why Frankenstein bothers."

"Maybe right *would* have been better," Jake murmured.

"We're armed," Cally hissed. "Shouldn't we take them?"

Jake deliberated. "Our first priority has got to be finding the others. We back up."

But now there were voices behind them, too: "He's not gonna be happy. He doesn't like surprises."

"I know how he feels," muttered Jake.

Cally tugged at his sleeve and pointed. A door, set back in the wall. Maybe a storeroom or somewhere equally useful in which to hide until the traffic cleared. "Shall we?"

"I think we'd better."

Cally activated the entry mechanism. The door slid open. She and Jake slid through.

Beyond, there was total darkness and absolute silence, both of which the two intruders might have welcomed. But there was something else, a presence. They were not alone.

Somehow, perhaps by their entry, lights were activated.

The lights were dim, red.

And Frankenstein's creations stood before them.

"Dr. Frankenstein, it is a pleasure to speak to you at last." The face that had appeared mere seconds ago on the giant viewing screen high on a wall gave nothing away about the physical identity of its owner. The man's true features were distorted by a mask that resembled a photographic negative of a human face, a constantly shifting gray-scale form. Lori gazed at it and realized it told her all that she needed to know. This guy and Frankenstein would get along just fine.

Indeed, she thought, *the way the doctor was preening himself right now, they'd probably end up getting married.*

"And to you," simpered Frankenstein, his white fingers tying and untying like bows, "a distinct privilege. But I am afraid you have the advantage. What am I to call you?"

"Names are unimportant," the anonymous face said. "Names are part of the ordered, rational society that we reject and despise. It is enough that we are agents of CHAOS, and chaos we will bring to all the world."

"An admirable aim," Frankenstein flattered. "And for that purpose, you seek to recruit my children, I hope?"

"That is what this communication will decide."

"So what sort of name is that, then? CHAOS." Ben thought it was time to draw attention to himself, hoping that Lori and Jennifer would join in. They had to keep either Frankenstein or the masked guy talking, to delay the demonstration and give something a chance to happen that might yet save them. "It stinks about as much as your attitude. What, don't tell us, your parents never understood you?"

That was all that Ben had time to say before Frankenstein gestured angrily to his ant-mutants, and they seized him, smothering his mouth. Lori and Jennifer tried to help but were themselves restrained.

But maybe Ben had done enough. "Who are these impudent young people?" The negative image flickered, shifted, as the agent behind the mask turned to examine Bond Team.

"Their names are also unimportant," said Frankenstein. "They are nobodies, fodder, wanderers in the woods who are now to be blessed with a new destiny and a new life. They are to be born anew to swell the family of Frankenstein."

"Release the boy. I want to talk with him for a moment."

Scarlet fury flushed Frankenstein's cheeks, but only briefly. He mastered it well. Grudgingly, he indicated that Ben should be allowed to speak.

As the mutant guards stepped away, the CHAOS agent directed his shadowy gaze on Ben.

"We are the Crusade for Havoc, Anarchy, and the Overthrow of Society," he intoned. "We are CHAOS. We are the future. We are *your* future."

"Big words for a guy who's too afraid to show his face," sneered Ben. "Why's that? The mask an improvement?"

The agent chuckled coldly. "Such refreshing defiance," he said. "I wonder whether it will last when Dr. Frankenstein's genetic genius begins to work on you. We will see — and soon."

Soon? Ben frowned. *Soon wasn't good.* He looked toward the corridor, tried to visualize Cally, Eddie, and Jake — yes, he'd even accept rescue from Daly, given the circumstances — the three of them charging into the lab with laser rifles blazing. Unfortunately for Ben, his eyes were realists. They refused to fantasize. If he and the girls were going to get out of this, they'd have to do it themselves, and Ben had only one card left to play.

But then someone did come rushing into the laboratory, one of Frankenstein's gray-suited goons, his uniform matching his expression, as if he had some bad news to report. And bad news to Frankenstein was good news to his captives.

They watched the man whisper in Frankenstein's ear. They

saw the mad doctor's countenance sour. Then he glanced across at them and, for the first time, there was puzzlement in his eyes, uncertainty, as though something had happened that he'd not considered possible.

The CHAOS agent detected it. "Is something wrong, Dr. Frankenstein?"

"Of course not. Of course not." He said it twice as if that would make the words doubly convincing. "A minor situation has arisen, that is all, of no concern to us here."

"Minor situations have a habit of becoming major ones," cautioned the man in the mask. "Such is the nature of chaos."

Frankenstein flinched at the implied criticism. He snapped orders, and the goon left the laboratory smartly. *Must be some sort of disturbance,* Ben reasoned, *and Daly and the others had to be at the bottom of it.* The increased signs of hopefulness on Lori and Jennifer's faces suggested that they thought so, too. The odds on their survival were improving.

Or not. "I assure you," Frankenstein informed the agent, "that I am absolutely in control of everything that transpires within my own laboratory."

"That is good," said the agent, "because CHAOS does not ally itself with incompetents."

"However," Frankenstein added, "there seems little point in further delaying the demonstration. Into the gene chamber with them. Now!"

And now it was. Ben wrested himself free of the insect limbs around him, lashed out at the ant-creatures, and yelled for Lori and Jennifer to do the same.

They tried, but they failed. There were too many of Frankenstein's children for them to overcome.

The door to the gene chamber was open.

"This latest strain of mutagenic gas," they could hear Franken-stein explaining, "is a further attempt to successfully combine snake and human DNA. I'm sure you'll find the experiment fas-cinating, and rather less stressful than our subjects, although they should take comfort from the knowledge that their suffer-ing will provide a valuable contribution to the scientific ad-vancement of mankind."

The door was closed. There was no escape.

"Prepare for activation." And Frankenstein was triumphant.

Jake and Cally swung their rifles into readiness. "If we're gonna go down," Jake gritted, "let's go down fighting."

"Wait!" A single voice from among the cluster of threaten-ing mutants.

Jake couldn't work out whether the command was directed at the creatures or at Cally and himself, but there was an au-thority in it that made everyone comply. The owner of the voice stepped forward. He was like nothing Jake had yet seen. The mutants had all been monstrous, but this one seemed some-how unfinished, incomplete. Its hide appeared to have been torn roughly, bloodily from a rhinoceros and sewn to the vic-tim's original skin, like metal plates grafted onto the flesh. Its fin-gers and feet were gnarled, almost tusked, and the final human details of the face, the eyes and mouth, peered out at the in-truders as if trapped behind armor. And now that Jake's eyes had adjusted to the light, he realized that the half-dozen or so other beings in the room were the same — half-men, half-beast, like sci-fi monsters with their makeup incomplete.

"Wait. Wait," the creature repeated, venturing ever closer.

Its arms were outstretched in a sign of apparently peaceful intent, but Cally wasn't sure that she wanted to trust it. Maybe this was some kind of trick. She glanced at Jake who seemed just as confused.

"That's far enough," he warned. "We know how to use these."

The mutant bowed its head resignedly, defeatedly. "Of course you do," it said, "and I know where you were taught."

"What?" Cally felt fear clamp around her heart. *What did the creature mean?*

"I know you. I know who you are." The mutant raised its head again as if to double-check. "Cally. Jake. Bond Team. I remember you."

"What are you talking about?" Jake's fingers were keen to fire the rifle, to end this increasingly bizarre conversation.

"You mean you don't recognize me? How is that possible?" Brittle, bitter laughter. "Will Challis. I'm Will Challis."

"No," breathed Cally. "You can't be. . . ."

The creature that had been Will Challis nodded its head, its armored hide grating like rusted hinges. "My last mission didn't go too well." More humorless laughter. "Frankenstein's mutants overpowered me, brought me here. I thought they were going to kill me. Instead, they did worse. They did this." Will looked down at himself in revulsion, then up at Jake and Cally as if in sudden hope. "But how did you find me? Are you part of a Spy High operation?"

"Not exactly." With the initial shock passing, Jake quickly considered new possibilities. "It's a long story, but we can't rely on Spy High for help. And listen, Will, three of our teammates have been taken by Frankenstein."

"To the gene chamber," Will Challis guessed desolately. "Then you've lost them."

"No way," said Jake. "We're gonna find them, we're gonna save them, and you're gonna help us. We don't know our way around this complex, Will, or where this gene chamber is, but I think maybe you might."

"I do."

"Then what are we waiting for?"

"The point," Will snapped. "What is the point? There's nothing we can do. Look at what they did to me, a mission veteran, and you're only first-years. The best you can do is to run, to get out."

Jake started forward angrily, but Cally stopped him with a hand on his arm. She spoke gently to what remained of Will Challis: "Will, why are you being kept here? The other creatures we've seen, they didn't seem able to speak; they were entirely savage. But you . . ."

"Oh, we're the failures," Will responded. "The gene gas Frankenstein uses to convert us can still be unpredictable. It mutated our bodies but had little effect on our minds. Those of us here can still think. Part of us is still human."

"Then be human now," Cally urged. "Help us, Will. Help our friends. Please."

Will Challis smiled bleakly and squared his bulky shoulders. "Why not? We're only being kept here for reprocessing or disposal. Neither seems a particularly attractive option. We'll help you, even if we don't stand a chance."

"There's always a chance," Jake insisted. "There's always a way. There's got to be."

"Maybe there is." Jake's conviction seemed to impress Will Challis in spite of himself. He stood taller, more like a man. For the first time since his capture, he began to think like a secret agent. "After a successful mutation, there's one process more. Frankenstein operates on his children and implants a computer chip in their skulls. The guards who bring us our food said so. It's how he controls the monsters he's made. If the signal can be disrupted, perhaps . . ."

"Right." Jake was tensed and ready. "Then let's start disrupting."

It was no good, pounding the glass with their fists, kicking at it with their bare feet. It probably wouldn't have been any good had they been wearing iron boots. The glass was superthick. The chamber was sealed. There was no way out.

"This is it." Lori felt herself trembling involuntarily. "There's nothing we can do." She turned to Ben.

Ben winked at her as if this were a movie script and he'd read the next page. "There's always something we can do," he said. "We can refuse to panic for starters." Frankenstein seemed to be explaining something to the CHAOS agent, but no sound entered the gene chamber from outside. That seemed to suit Ben's purpose perfectly. "Particularly," he grinned, "when at least one forward-thinking secret agent has a nitronail on the middle finger of his right hand."

"Still no sign of the others, though." Jennifer was watching the corridor.

"With any luck, we won't need the others," said Ben, a little disappointed that Jennifer and Lori weren't awestruck by his foresight. But no matter. In just a few moments, he would have proved his worth as leader of Bond Team by blasting their way out of the very first fate-worse-than-death trap that they'd encountered in the field. Now, while the good doctor was still distracted, Ben ripped off the nitronail and slapped it to the glass side of the gene chamber.

"Stand back. Behind me," he said protectively. "And get ready for the fight of our lives."

The nitronail exploded.

But the sheer walls of the gene chamber did not.

A few thin, spidery cracks remained, but no gaping hole, no shattered glass. No exit.

Precious little hope.

Outside, Frankenstein waved to his prisoners with the worms of his fingers. At least, they were spared the giggle.

Ben lunged at the damaged glass desperately, rammed his shoulder against it, thumped it with all his weight. "Maybe it's weakened enough. . . ." But he didn't believe it.

"Jake, Cally, someone, come on . . ." Jennifer was pleading, and this time Ben could hardly blame her.

Frankenstein threw a switch. He applauded his own action.

A noise. A steady hissing sound, like that of a tangle of snakes.

"What's that? What is it?" But Jennifer already knew.

Lori held Ben more tightly as it pumped through the vents in the floor and slithered slyly toward them.

The gene gas.

Hold on, Jake was thinking as he hurtled through corridors. *Jennifer, Lori, Ben*, he was thinking, *Hold on. Whatever Frankenstein is doing to you, don't give up. We're close, Cally and me. We're close and we're coming.*

They knew their way, now. They had allies. Will Challis

and his mutant cell mates were with them. They had something like a plan, at least a hint of Frankenstein's possible weakness. They had a chance. And nothing yet had stood in their path. Surely, the gene chamber had to be close. Maybe this was going to be easier than expected. Maybe there'd be no opposition at all. Maybe —

And then they burst into the room where the others had first awoken, the space that looked like an operating room. And then Jake saw the forces that were lined up against them.

Time to give up on the maybes.

A barrage of laser blasts tore into their advancing ranks, killing one of the mutants instantly and wounding two others. "Cover!" Jake cried, throwing himself to the ground. Cally followed suit, finding what protection she could by a bank of computers. "Get behind us!" Jake yelled to Will Challis and the others. "We'll protect you!" He should have said they'd *try* to. Only two laser rifles against those fired by a whole squad of Frankenstein's men who were spread out across the far side of the room as though they'd been anticipating just such an incursion.

"I think we're outnumbered!" Cally called out.

"You don't say." Jake chose to look on the bright side. "All the more targets for us to hit." He and Cally were both very good at target practice. And they started to prove it, picking off opponents as laser blasts sparked and crackled around them. Frankenstein's goons were merely the hired help; Jake and Cally were students of Spy High.

But even though they were better shots, they could not afford to stay pinned down for long.

Will Challis yelled in Jake's ear above the sizzle of the laser fire. "Aim at the computers! This is where Frankenstein operates on the mutants! Their control chips are linked to the computers. Destroy them!"

Jake nodded that he understood. "Cally!" he instructed. "Keep me covered!"

"What?" *Easier said than done,* thought Cally anxiously, as the heat of the enemy's fire singed her hair. But she trusted Jake, even when he started shooting at the console. The result was lots of flames and explosions, but exactly how it was going to help them, she could not guess. And it looked like things were about to get worse.

Frankenstein's men were signaling. It seemed as though Jake's actions were forcing them to change tactics.

The creatures that rampaged into the room did not need to be issued orders. They already knew what to do, as a predator instinctively knows its prey. A mutant with bat wings. A mutant with an ape's head. It was like old times again, and now that Cally was armed and now that she knew what to expect, she looked forward to reacquainting herself with the creatures from the forest. She remembered the bodies of the hunters. But, as the mutants launched themselves in a murderous assault, could she bring them all down?

Maybe she wouldn't need to. With a yell of anguish and hatred and pain, Will Challis surged ahead and charged the attackers. His fellow mutants also joined the fray. The howls and roars and shrieks of the creatures reverberated in the room like the cries of a thousand maniacs. Then came the sickening crunch of bodies in merciless, unforgiving combat, the fatal flash of claw and tooth and talon, bright sprays of blood from wounds slashed wide, panic and pain pounding at the walls, the air, and then the wild moans of the dying.

Cally now fired at Frankenstein's creatures as well as his men. Smoke billowed into the air, stinging her eyes. She only half-registered that her thigh was grazed and bleeding.

The bank of computers erupted around her.

It was carnage, confusion. Despite Will's attack, the creatures kept on coming. Sooner or later, the laser blasts would not miss. They couldn't hold out. It was not possible.

It was up to Eddie now.

The tree ahead of him burst into flames, so near that Eddie could feel the heat on his skin. He veered to avoid it, scorching his leg but still able to ride, still out in front of his one remaining pursuer.

Didn't this guy ever give up?

To be fair, Frankenstein's other lackeys hadn't exactly given up, either. It was just a little difficult to continue the chase when your SkyBike had crashed, and you were left vainly shaking your fist after your intended victim. Eddie would have waved back just to be polite, but he'd been otherwise preoccupied.

Still was.

This last guy was like a limpet. He seemed to be locked on to Eddie's bike, and he kept getting closer with those laser bolts all the time. Eddie couldn't outrace him, didn't seem able to outmaneuver him. So what could he do? The others were relying on him. He had to reach the control post no matter what.

Behind him, his pursuer was gaining, pinpointing his laser on Eddie one final time. Before him was the tallest, straightest tree he had ever seen. Eddie put the two together and hoped his timing was good enough.

He increased his speed. Collision course.

His pursuer fired. Eddie forced his bike upward, rearing recklessly into the sky.

The bolt blazed underneath him, struck the tree, and ignited it.

Eddie's pursuer had no time to compensate. His bike could not avoid the flaming trunk. He threw himself off it. There was an explosion. The tree wasn't having a good day.

But Eddie was. He was the last man riding, and the control post was almost within sight. He felt that he could allow himself to gloat a bit. To take a backward glance at the fallen goon who was dragging himself to his feet.

Even as he did so Eddie thought of the race back at Spy High. On a SkyBike traveling at top speed and with trees around, you had to look where you were going. He was being a jerk. The others were relying on him.

Eddie's head snapped round.

Too late.

CHAPTER ELEVEN

They clung together as if the contact might defend them from the gas.

It didn't.

Lori stared in horror as it felt its way blindly across the floor of the gene chamber, curling, coiling toward them, reaching out with noxious fingers. It wound around her ankles, and she screamed. She couldn't help herself. The gas tingled as it seeped into her pores, as it rubbed against her bare legs like a witch's cat.

Jennifer was whining softly. "I can feel it. I can feel it in me."

"Don't swallow it." Ben was grasping at straws as the gas rose like a deadly tide to his waist. "Whatever you do, hold your breath. Help might still be on the way. The others . . . or Grant . . . somebody . . ." He took deep gulps of unpoisoned air. Ben could hold his breath a long time.

But Lori felt her mind drifting. It wasn't an unpleasant sensation. She was somewhere green and peaceful, and her senses were alive in a way they'd never been before. She tried to raise her arms, but she had no arms; and she tried to call out, but her tongue only flickered in the grass. Inside her body, her cells began to change.

The gas lapped at their shoulders, their chins. It would wash over them soon, and they would drown in it.

And the desert heat was on Jennifer's twining back, and she writhed among the rocks, and she moved on her belly in search of food.

The gas rolled over them, smothering, suffocating.

Ben held his breath. *Lori and Jennifer were like ghosts now, phantoms in the fog. How long before the process was irreversible? How long before their genes mutated forever? It couldn't end like this. Where was the glory if it ended like this? What would have been the point?*

He felt his lungs constrict, his throat tighten. He felt himself slipping away. There were glimpses of jungle, of rivers, and he sensed himself floating on their surfaces even as he sunk to the chamber floor, his face pressed against the glass. He could still break it. If only he could concentrate . . .

And was something happening out there? Blurs of commotion through the mist and haze. It didn't matter anyway. He couldn't hold his breath any longer. His body was betraying him.

Ben parted his lips to taste the gene gas.

Cally parted her lips to cry out, but she didn't have time. The wolf-mutant was on her in a second, the force of its attack knocking her on her side. The laser rifle fell from her grasp, and she couldn't retrieve it.

The stench of the creature was in her nostrils, making her gag. Saliva drooled from its jagged mouth as razored teeth snapped at her throat. Cally chopped at the mutant's own throat, always a potentially vulnerable and disabling spot, but she couldn't get the leverage to make her blow count. Claws raked at her skin. Her eyes and the mutant's were as close as lovers', but she saw only hatred there, madness and rage. She'd always hoped that the last thing she'd ever see would somehow be beautiful. Seemed it wasn't meant to be.

And then the mutant howled. And then it let her go and reared up on its hind legs, tearing at its skull like a child unwrapping a present. It staggered. It reeled. The other mutants were doing the same. Cally didn't ask why. She snatched up her laser rifle and fired at her assailant. The wolf-mutant didn't have to worry anymore.

"It's working!" Jake was shouting gleefully. "We've done it! The implants are blown. Let's see if Frankenstein finds them as easy to order around now!"

The doctor's own men seemed to doubt it. For the first time, they ceased fire on Cally and Jake and trained their weapons on the mutants instead. Just in case.

Just in case turned out to be just as well.

With a collective cry, the creatures turned toward their former masters — turned against their former masters. Revenge, it seemed, was an emotion even Frankenstein's children could understand.

The ant-creatures who waited dutifully at Frankenstein's side screeched in sudden pain, clutching at their misshapen heads as their warrior brethren had done.

Frankenstein and his technicians watched in alarm.

"What does this mean, Frankenstein?" asked the CHAOS agent. "What of your assertion that you have the situation under control?"

One of the technicians, realizing what was about to happen, darted for the corridor. He didn't get there. An ant-mutant seized him and twisted him back. The crack of the man's neck snapping was like a starter's gun. Everybody ran.

"Control," Frankenstein observed, "is a relative term."

His fingers fluttered helplessly as his mutants encircled him.

* * *

The battle between Frankenstein's men and Frankenstein's children was ending in the only way possible: Laser fire had cut down many of the creatures, but those that remained were berserk with bloodlust, not caring whether they lived or died. The same could not be said of the doctor's lackeys. As the first of them were brought down and sliced open by claws and teeth and tusks, the others teetered on the brink of retreat. Renewed fire from Jake and Cally gave them no choice.

Frankenstein's lackeys fled. With the mutants after them, it was unlikely they'd get very far.

"Come on!" Jake urged. "Cally! We've still got work to do."

"No, Jake. Look." Cally knelt by a body on the floor. It was the body that had once been Will Challis, graduate of Spy High and former leader of Bond Team.

Jake knelt, too, his eyes quickly registering that there was no hope. Deep wounds had brought Will peace. "He's dead, Cal." Jake put his arm around her shoulders and squeezed consolingly. "Jen and the others might still be alive. We have to leave him."

"I know." She lightly touched the bridge of human skin between Will Challis's sightless eyes. "Thank you."

They were on their feet again. The day was not yet over.

But for Frankenstein, it was close. He was surrounded. The ant-mutants had been joined by several other creatures, their fur and claws already matted with blood. Frankenstein was not eager to add to it. He hoped they'd listen to reason as they advanced upon him.

"Stop!" he appealed desperately. "Listen to me. Listen to me! You don't want to harm me. You can't. I made you. I molded you. Without me, you would not exist. I am your father and you are all my children, my beautiful children. You cannot turn against me!"

Cally and Jake arrived in time to witness Dr. Frankenstein's final moments. His final words were almost pitiful: "I deserve your love!" And then the mutants, showing Frankenstein exactly what they thought he deserved, fell upon him, dragging him to the floor, ripping and rending the air with their fury.

"Cally!" alerted Jake. "Forget Frankenstein. The chamber!"

The glass chamber was filled with gas. Still and silent forms were inside. But it could not be too late. *Please, not too late*, they thought.

Jake and Cally fired their laser rifles in unison. Together, they let out a great cry of triumph.

The gene chamber had shattered.

Ben coughed up the filthy gas from his lungs and hoped the rest of the contents of his stomach wouldn't come up with it. He felt dizzy, lightheaded. It was like the first time he'd tried to smoke, years ago as a child. That experience had put him off tobacco for life, and this one wasn't exactly going to have him lining up outside gene chambers everywhere, begging to be let in.

But at least — yes, with trembling fingers, he felt his skin (not scales) and his tongue (unforked) — at least the nightmare of imminent mutation was over. He knew who he was, and he was still human. The gene gas was clearing up, dissipating, now that the chamber that had contained it was ruptured. Help had come in the nick of time, but from what source?

Ben propped himself up on weakened elbows. Cally and Jake, he saw them. He also saw Jennifer and Lori groaning alongside him.

Lori. Ben very much wanted to hold Lori at this point. Fortunately for him, the feeling was mutual.

Cally and Jake rushed to their teammates' assistance. It didn't escape Cally's attention that Jake made straight for Jennifer. She wouldn't have expected him to be quite so attentive to Ben, obviously, or even to Lori, but this went beyond comforting. It meant something more. Cally remembered the forest, what she'd thought: that her chance with Jake would come. *What chance? No chance.*

Best to cover up her own feelings by turning to Ben and Lori. "Are you two okay?"

"We will be," Ben said.

"Sorry we didn't get here sooner, but we ran into trouble, mutant style."

"Where's Eddie?" Lori looked for him worriedly.

"It's okay. He's SkyBiking for help."

Ben struggled to his feet. It was time he started acting like team leader again. "And Frankenstein? Dr. Averill, I mean."

"It's all right," Cally said. "We know who Dr. Averill was."

"Was?"

"I think those bits of him over there suggest 'was,' Ben."

Ben and Lori both looked. The remains were not pretty, but they could tell they were Frankenstein's. What was left of the fingers gave it away. "Don't waste any pity on him, Lori," Ben advised, knowing her tendencies. "Remember what he tried to do to us."

"And what he did to Will Challis," Jake added, helping Jennifer up.

"Will Challis? What are you talking about?"

"We'll tell you when we're out of here." Jake glanced around.

"Looks like any surviving mutants have flown the coop. Shall we follow suit?"

"After you, Jake," said Ben. "You seem to know your way around." He grinned. "If you can let go of Jennifer for a second."

"Who's that?"

Cally had wandered away from the others a little and was now pointing to the screen from which the CHAOS agent, who was all but forgotten, still looked on. It was difficult to tell what he was feeling about the recent turn of events. The masked face showed no expression.

Ben advanced on the screen. "Not turning out quite the way you'd planned, huh, Mr. CHAOS man?"

"I wouldn't say that." The negative mask glittered in what might have been a smile. "It has been most informative, thanks to you and your friends. It is always wise for an organization such as ours to be aware of any weakness in our potential allies, just as it is to be alert to any strengths in our potential foes."

"What do you mean?"

"You, young man. You and the rest of your group. You are more than you appear to be, that much is clear. Perhaps, one day, we will find out what." The agent seemed to sigh. "But for now, you have served us well. Dr. Frankenstein was obviously not a worthy partner for us even had he lived, but we have other plans. The world will be hearing from CHAOS very soon. Very soon indeed."

The screen flickered and went blank.

"My God," breathed Jake. "I don't believe it."

"What?" His teammates shuddered at the prospect of new danger.

"He didn't even say good-bye."

Lori laughed, playfully slapping Jake's arm. "Who needs Eddie when we've got you, Jake?"

"Who needs Eddie at all?" Jennifer added, possibly still holding a grudge from the judo match.

"Don't be like that," said Cally, who was perhaps developing a different kind of resentment. "Eddie should be here. He ought to be a part of this."

"I guess Cally's right," said Ben. "This has turned out to be our first real mission: Bond Team's baptism of fire. And we've done it; we've proved ourselves. Forget Stromfeld and all that computer-generated make-believe. We've just fought a real maniac in the real world, and we've won. Frankenstein's dead. We're heroes."

One day, Jake thought, *Ben's permanent condition of self-congratulation would become terminal, and then there'd be a vacancy at the top for leader of Bond Team. But not, perhaps, today.*

On second thought . . .

Suddenly, the screens in the gene chamber lit up. All but two seemed to be showing other areas of the Frankenstein Factory: the labs and the lodge.

"What? What's going on?" Cally said disconcertedly.

The final pair of screens. On one: a missile launching from its silo, and beneath it, a map with the missile blinking in red at the start of its journey. On the other: an all too familiar face and all too familiar squirming white fingers.

"Oh, dear," lamented Frankenstein. "If you're watching this, whoever you are, it means I must be dead, and you were probably responsible. Never mind. I have a surprise for you." That wretched high-pitched giggle again. "You'll soon be joining me."

They all gasped.

"How . . ." Lori began.

Cally was frowning. "He must have recorded this earlier, to be activated if his heartbeat stopped or something."

"Yeah, well, he couldn't very well do it now, could he?" snorted Ben unhelpfully. "Not with his heart about ten feet from his head."

"Quiet, both of you, and listen." Jake hadn't taken his eyes off the screen.

"I expect you're watching the missile," Frankenstein said. "My final blessing to the human race. A gene bomb, filled to the brim with a generous helping of the insect strain of my gas, enough to give a city full of people a whole new outlook on life. What wonderful workers they'll make in just a few minutes' time. Perhaps you might like to stay and watch. There's a camera attached to the nose cone of the bomb."

"Can we stop it?" Jennifer asked.

"No 'can we' about it," said Jake. "We've *got* to stop it. We're the only ones who can."

Cally felt the pressure of the others' eyes upon her. She thought of Stromfeld. She thought of failure. She thought of the possible millions of people who, although they didn't know it, were about to be relying on her to save their lives.

"Oh, and don't think I've forgotten you, either," the doctor continued. "I'd rather my lab not fall into the hands of those who might not appreciate my work appropriately, no doubt yourself or selves included. So, just about now, you ought to be feeling the first shock wave of a series of explosions, which, sadly, will mean the destruction of all you survey." As if on cue, they heard a distant rumble. The walls trembled, as if in fear of what was about to happen to them. "Not so sadly, this almost certainly means that you won't be able to leave my premises safely. In fact, I rather feel your fate here is sealed."

"We've got to get out of here," Jennifer urged.

"We can't." Jake restrained her. "Not until we've stopped the gene bomb. That's our first priority."

"I'm open to suggestions," said Ben.

"Leave it to me." Cally stepped forward. "After all, I'm supposed to be the techno-wizard, aren't I? Or witch?" She eyed Ben steadily. "The bomb is my responsibility."

Ben nodded grimly. "Prove it."

Cally only prayed that she could. She seated herself quickly at the console beneath the display of the bomb, ordered herself to ignore its close resemblance to the control panel in the Stromfeld program. Even if it looked the same, it wasn't, and even if she felt just as stressed as she'd been in virtual reality, if not more so, she couldn't allow the same outcome. The gene bomb could not be permitted to detonate.

Unlike Frankenstein's lodge. The lab rocked with several blistering explosions, each one louder and nearer than the last, like a barrage of artillery trying to find its range. Screen after screen depicted eruptions of fire. The cell where Will Challis had been kept. The lounge with the painting of the centaur.

"Hurry," Jennifer muttered, although the same sentiment was on everyone's expression. "Cal, hurry."

Cally's fingers were doing what they could, blurring across the keys. Information was displayed before her: codes, clues, the coyness of a system intent on keeping secrets. Coax the system, that was the way to do it, tease it, beguile it, be sensitive to it, attune yourself to it. You had to become part of it to understand it. You had to be like Cally's own chameleon unit, to think like the computer. It was the only way.

The flashing dot of the gene bomb arched down toward a doomed population. From the nose-cone camera, clouds thinned and cleared.

"And now," Frankenstein continued, "a few words for posterity, I think, entitled 'Dr. Averill Frankenstein: Genius Misunderstood.'"

"He doesn't even shut up when he's dead," Ben moaned.

Cally shut out the sounds. Before, she'd let herself be rushed. She'd remained too human. Now, Cally felt herself becoming one with the computer. It shyly let her in. The guidance systems of the bomb all but belonged to her.

"You can't just blow it up in the air," Lori realized. "The gene gas: It could still spread. Cally . . ."

"I know." She felt tranquil, serene. The systems were bending to her will. She was one with them. Just a few seconds more . . .

Land loomed on the flight path of the bomb. A coastal city, the ocean wide and vast beyond it. The bleeping was even louder now, building to a crescendo.

"Cally . . . ," Ben urged helplessly.

What had she said to Eddie? *"Stromfelds exist, don't they? Madmen and their crazy schemes."* And here was Frankenstein's bomb, so close to success. *"One day, real lives will depend on us."* They did. That day was now. *"And what happens then . . . ?"*

The screen was screaming. The bomb was swooping. Cally remembered something else. Being too slow. But not this time. Not when it truly mattered.

"Look!" Jake cried out, with pride in his voice. "The bomb's changing course!"

It was indeed. Cally reared the missile up, sent it shooting past its intended target, high above the heads of Frankenstein's intended victims, plunged it harmlessly into the depths of the sea, and let it sink and drown and be forgotten.

There were whoops and howls and cries of delight all around her. Lori hugged her. Jake did, too. "I knew you could do it, Cal," he said. Even Ben looked suitably impressed. And she heard herself laughing out loud, laughing with a wild relief.

Because what did Eddie say to her after "What happens then?" *"Then we'll get it right."*

Amen to that, Cally thought. *Amen to that.*

"Now, what was that part about getting out of here?" Ben said.

"Not yet." Jake pointed his laser rifle at the screen where Frankenstein was still droning on about the benefits of genetic manipulation. "I think we've just about heard enough from you, Dr. Frankenstein." He fired once. The screen exploded. "Now I'm ready to leave."

The virtual scenarios back at Spy High meant they at least understood the technique of escape from a burning building, but VR didn't come close to matching the actual heat generated by the inferno that Frankenstein's lodge was swiftly becoming. If they managed to survive without being burned to a crisp, Ben made a mental note to bring that up with the programmers.

Through the blazing labs, the five members of Bond Team ran, keeping to the center of each space as much as possible, a hand on the teammate in front of them so that in the sometimes black and billowing smoke, they would not be separated. Jake was in the lead and Cally in the rear by virtue of the fact that they had fought their way from the residential part of the lodge to the labs. Not even Ben protested his relegation to the role of follower this once.

In the operating room, only Cally spared a glance for the fallen form of Will Challis. *It could have been me*, she thought, *it could have been any of us. Could still be one day.* As flames rippled along the walls, as the walls themselves seemed to sway and topple, the stinging in her eyes came from more than the smoke. They'd been lucky this time. Their training and their wits had been sufficient to save them — just barely. But next time? And the time after that? When would their luck run out?

She must have loosened her hold on Lori's shoulder, as the other girl was suddenly turning to her in alarm. "Cal? You all right?"

Cally squeezed Lori's shoulder once more and nodded. *For now*, she thought, *and maybe now was all that mattered.*

The lodge still burned. Fire lashed from shattered windows and gaping doorways like a raging beast struggling to run free. The building was engulfed, a single monumental funeral pyre for the mad dreams of Dr. Averill Frankenstein.

The five of them watched the conflagration from a safe distance, gasping, exhausted but still alive. And they realized that they were holding onto each other, holding each other tightly, close, like they were truly a team at last.

"It's a pity we couldn't save anything," Ben said. "I know he was sick and twisted, but Frankenstein was still doing pioneering work. Who knows what kind of applications it might have had in the right hands?"

"Trouble is," Lori remarked, "whose hands are the right hands? Maybe it's better this way."

"Well, Benny boy," grinned Jake, "if you want to dash back and look for a copy of Frankenstein's notes, I guess you have about half a minute before the roof caves in."

"It's going now!" cried Jennifer, and the roof of the lodge collapsed amid an eruption of heat and sparks.

"I think I'll pass," said Ben.

"Some camping trip this turned out to be," said Cally.

"Listen! What's that?" Jennifer suddenly wheeled, tensed, the throb of magnetic engines somewhere behind them.

"It's all right." Jake relaxed. "I think they used to call it the cavalry."

It was Eddie. He was on a SkyBike, and he wasn't alone. About a dozen rangers from the control post were with him, fully armed and tight-lipped as though they were expecting danger. Eddie landed his bike and dismounted. His teammates joined him.

"What happened, speed king?" Jake demanded good-humoredly. "What took you so long? Distracted by a pretty face?"

"This?" Eddie said nonchalantly, indicating a cut and bruise above his left eye. "It's nothing. I got into an argument with a tree is all."

"And you should see the tree," Lori anticipated.

"Nice one. Yeah," Eddie approved. "Thanks for caring, though."

"We're just glad to see you, Eddie." Cally had flung her arms around him before she'd even realized she was going to. "Now we're all back together. Just as it should be."

"You said it, Cal. One thing, though." Eddie stared at the fiery ruin of the Frankenstein Factory. "What did I miss?"

CHAPTER TWELVE

"Children," sneered Stromfeld. "They send children to distract me."

"Yeah, that's right," said Eddie, "and have you ever thought of changing your scriptwriter?"

"Besides," added Ben pointedly, "think what trouble you'd be in if they had sent adults."

"Trouble? Did you say trouble?" This latest version of Stromfeld seemed to be a little hard of hearing. "It will be a cold day in hell before impudent puppies such as yourselves can disturb the plans of Stromfeld."

"Get those thermals on then," advised Jake, "or are you telling us that the shrinking ray that we cleverly got to backfire on you isn't having any effect?"

"Impossible. Impossible." Stromfeld glanced desperately between the faces of the six members of Bond Team who encircled him, who dared to surround him here, in the very nerve center of his operation. How had it come to this? He was Stromfeld. He could not be defeated. And if he escaped now, there could still be a chance. He tried to force his way past Lori and Jennifer. They pushed him back easily. He was already shorter than them, and getting smaller all the time.

"I don't think so," said Jennifer with venom. "The only way you're going is *down*."

"You know," Lori considered, "I think I liked him better when he was fat."

"I've never liked him," said Cally, and the others could see that she meant it.

"No sweat," said Eddie helpfully. "I don't think you're going to have to put up with him for much longer, Cal."

Because now Stromfeld barely came up to their shoulders, and rather than stopping, or even slowing down, the process seemed to be accelerating. He began to wail as the floor rose up to meet him.

"It was a good plan, Stromfeld," conceded Ben. "Use your shrinking ray to reduce the world's population to the size of ants. You'd have had godlike power then, all right, ruling over a race of insects. But you made one mistake in your calculations, didn't you? You didn't think about Ben Stanton — you didn't think about Bond Team."

"Nice one, Ben," said Eddie. "You write that yourself?"

"No, no!" Stromfeld was at the level of their waists now. His voice was starting to squeak. "It can't end like this! I am Stromfeld. I cannot . . ."

"I think you can," said Jake coldly.

He was at their knees now, shrinking, the size of a puppet without strings. "Help me! Help me!" He let out tiny squeals of fear, but Bond Team did not move. "I'll give you anything, anything! Only help me! Please!" Now he was at their ankles, and smaller still. Stromfeld scurried on the floor like an agitated ant.

"Well, we can't let him get away," said Jake, "even at that size. Anybody want to do the honors?"

Ben looked like he did, but Cally was quicker. "I do," she stated. "Stromfeld owes me."

And she stamped her foot down, twisted her sole on the floor. It felt good.

"Be careful you don't track that on the carpet," said Eddie.

"Well, well, well." Suddenly, Corporal Keene appeared. "So

you finally got it right." He didn't look particularly pleased, although he didn't look displeased, either.

"Stromfeld squashed," Ben said. "I assume that's a pass."

"It's a pass," said Keene. "Looks like we'll be seeing you next term, after all."

It was the last night of the semester, and Christmas was in the air. Deveraux Academy (the part of it that was above ground, anyway) was dutifully decorated with tinsel and lights. Eddie had appropriated virtually the entire stock of mistletoe and had, allegedly, been gargling mouthwash for a week. Maybe he would have been better advised to change his deodorant, too, because the girls he approached with his bouquet of mistletoe still headed for the nearest exit as if he were advancing with an ax.

There was a party that night, and the rec room was bursting at the seams with festive food and drink. Favorite yuletide records played, among them the time-honored classics from the 2050s or even earlier. "There's something wrong with this old recording of Grant's," someone had been heard to say. "'White Christmas' by a guy called Bing Crosby? *Bing?* That's not a name, it's a sound effect. And anyway, it can't be playing right. Nobody could have sung that low naturally."

Ben didn't care whether there was music or not. Short of a full-scale nuclear attack on Deveraux Academy, nothing could spoil the evening for him. Leader of Bond Team, Lori on his arm, a pass in the Stromfeld program and the highest first-semester grade-point-average since the inception of Spy High — Santa had already been good to Benjamin T. Stanton Jr. this year, and he didn't think he was being unrealistic in anticipating even better things to come.

"You look happy tonight," Lori said.

"And why not?" Ben laughed. "Full of the holiday spirit, that's me. Peace and goodwill to all men." Then he spotted Simon Macey. "With one exception."

"No, Ben." Lori pulled at his sleeve. "No trouble. Not tonight."

Ben kissed her. "Who said anything about trouble, gorgeous? I just want to wish old Simon a very merry Christmas." And he kissed her again before Lori could object further. If only he could think of a similarly foolproof technique to keep Jake Daly quiet.

Simon Macey saw Ben coming. He didn't even pretend to look friendly.

Ben, on the other hand, did. "Simon, Simon —" opening his arms expansively, like a welcoming host — "good to see you. Merry Christmas."

"Get lost, Stanton."

"Come on, don't be like that. I just came over to thank you for the card."

"What card?"

"The Christmas card. The one you sent wishing me all the best. You know, congratulating me on passing Stromfeld and finishing the year at the top in just about everything. The one where you apologized abjectly for thinking you could, in any way, ever be a match for Ben Stanton. You know, Simon, *that* card."

"You're mad. One of these days —"

"Yeah? One of these days what, Simon? 'Cause next term the inter-team competition really shifts into high gear, doesn't it? And it'll be Bond Team versus Solo Team, and I think we both know what the outcome of that'll be, don't we? Me, I can't wait."

"Go away. Just go away."

"Sure. There's a funny smell around here, anyway. I think it's mediocrity. Before I do, though . . ."

"What?" Simon snapped, edging to the brink of violence.

"Happy New Year."

"You enjoyed that, didn't you?" Lori scolded, having deftly maneuvered Ben to the other side of the rec room. It had been so petty, so childish. Sometimes she wondered what she saw in Ben, although she tried to keep those times to a minimum.

"I did, actually." Ben was immune to criticism. "And now I want to celebrate with our teammates. Where is everybody?"

"Cally's here." She was there, but was sitting by herself, looking as if the holidays were just about to end rather than begin. "And Eddie's over there." He was waving his mistletoe like it was some sort of magic wand that knew only one spell, but was an expert at it — how to make girls disappear.

"That's not good enough," Ben disapproved. "We should all be here. All the other teams are. Where's Jennifer?"

"Still in our room," Lori supplied. "Said she wasn't feeling very well."

"And what about Daly? I'm feeling so good tonight I can even put up with Daly."

"Jake? I don't know." Lori seemed faintly puzzled. "I haven't seen him. . . ."

There was no answer, although he knew she was in there.

Of course, he could just walk away now, beat a furtive, slightly guilty retreat, and be glad that no one had come by to see him standing lamely outside her door. Or he could knock again. He knew she was in there. He also knew how much effort it had taken him to even come here, to take that chance with Jen that she'd hardly encouraged. If he simply gave up now, he'd be a coward.

So he knocked again, more loudly this time, in a I'm-not-leaving-until-you've-at-least-admitted-that-I'm-here kind of way. "Jennifer, are you in there?" He knew that she was.

"Who is it?" Her voice reluctant and resentful.

"It's me. Jake." If she said "Jake who?" he'd admit defeat now. But she didn't say anything. He gave another prompt: "Can I come in?"

"I don't know. *Can* you?"

Jake took that as a grudging "yes" and tried the door. It opened easily enough. It was only in the way if they wanted it to be.

Jennifer was sitting cross-legged on her bed. The holiday spirit had so far seemed to elude her: She could have appeared in the dictionary under "miserable." In front of her, she held the photograph of her family, tenderly, as if she were cradling an egg.

"What do you want, Jake?" Her tone was not encouraging.

"Well, the party's in full swing . . . getting that way . . . I thought . . . I wondered where you were and if, well . . ."

"I don't like parties," Jennifer said bluntly. "Too many people pretending to be having a good time. I'm not good at pretend-ing."

"Yeah, but the last night of the semester?" Jake ventured fur-ther into the room. He saw the stoop of Jennifer's shoulders and wanted to touch them. "You shouldn't be alone on the last night."

"We're all alone. What difference does it make, trying to cover it up by being in a crowd?"

"Well, if it doesn't make a difference, why not come to the party anyway?"

He almost got a smile for that, thin and bitter as it was. "You don't give up, do you?"

"No, I don't. Come on. I hear Keene's going to be turning up as Santa Claus later, and that's got to be worth seeing." Jake parodied the corporal's voice: "So, little boy, give me your name, rank, number, and what present you want delivered by 0600 Christmas morning. And that's Santa *sir* to you."

There was another near smile, as Jennifer returned the photograph to the head of her bed.

"Your family?" Jake asked. "You going home for Christmas, Jen?"

She looked at him directly for the first time, and her eyes were cold. "I'll come with you to the party, Jake," she said, "so long as you give it a rest with the twenty-questions routine."

"Whatever you say." And whatever Jennifer said, it was unlikely to prevent Jake's smile from splitting the top of his head open.

She didn't stop trying, though. "And I don't want you reading too much into this. It doesn't mean anything. Don't get ideas. I warned you in the forest. . . ."

"It's all right, Jen. Don't panic." Jake raised his hands in mock surrender. "I'm a Domer, remember? We don't get ideas."

But he was lying. And it felt better than the truth.

In one suite of rooms at Deveraux Academy, there was no trace of Christmas, no trace of the passage of time at all. This was Deveraux's room. And Senior Tutor Elmore Grant was there.

Jonathan Deveraux called him in to report at the oddest moments.

"I'm afraid there's nothing else on CHAOS at this time, sir," Grant said, "no further information, despite the IGC working at full stretch."

"Hmm. My own researchers, too, have failed to uncover anything of use. But we need to remain vigilant, Grant. I sense that CHAOS will not stay silent for long." Grant nodded his agreement. "Well, simply learning of their existence has proved a valuable additional benefit to Bond Team's foray into the Wildscape, has it not? And some compensation for the loss of Agent Challis."

"Indeed, sir."

"You sound skeptical, Grant. Do you still doubt we did the right thing, when their exposure to genuine danger has clearly been the making of Bond Team?"

"Of course not, sir —" Grant braved a "but" — "but I do feel that sometimes, these days, it's possible that you forget how young these new students are, how —"

"Be careful, Grant." Deveraux's voice sounded a note of caution. "I forget nothing, not even how old *you* are."

"Yes, sir."

"But what are we even discussing? Bond Team has passed Stromfeld. Your choices have been a credit to you, Grant. All's well. Go and enjoy the party. It's Christmas, is it not?"

"Yes, sir."

"Then a merry Christmas to you, Grant."

"Yes, sir. Thank you, sir." But he still thought Deveraux was wrong.

* * *

It was the last straw for Cally when Jake entered the rec room with Jennifer. He didn't exactly have his arm around her, but he was at her side like a magnet to metal. And he looked like he wanted to be. Ben and Lori waved them over to where they and Cally were sitting. "I'm feeling a toast coming on," Ben warned. "Where's Eddie?" Cally said she'd fetch him.

There he was, with his mistletoe and his prepuckered lips. Still no takers, not even in pity. *And was this going to be in pity? Or to show Jake that she really didn't need him? Or did she really like Eddie after all?* Maybe she'd know afterward.

"Eddie?"

"Oh, hi, Cal. I don't suppose . . ." He raised the mistletoe meekly.

"Do suppose," she said. "Do very suppose."

And she kissed him. And she meant it. And it lasted awhile.

"Did you . . . ?" Eddie seemed dazed. "I'm a little bit overcome here, but did you really just . . . ?"

"I really did," grinned Cally, "and who's for second helpings?"

"Excuse me just one moment." Eddie turned and yelled across to Simon Macey. "Hey, Macey, give yourself a chance." He flung the mistletoe, and it bounced off Simon's head. "Don't think I'll be needing that any more. Will I, Cal?"

"You tell me." *So what if it wasn't going to be perfect?* she thought. *That didn't stop it from being good.*

"Hey, everybody! Everybody!" Someone charged into the rec room. "It's snowing outside!"

"Snow," Ben snorted. "That's exciting. Now if I could just have a second . . ."

"Don't think so," said Jake, "'cause to a Domer like me, snow *is* exciting. I've never been out in it before." Masses of students were already rushing outside.

Jennifer, Cally, and Eddie eagerly followed Jake. Lori clearly wanted to go, too.

"But what about the toast?" Ben objected.

Lori dragged him to his feet. "Come on, Ben. Let it burn."

And it *was* snowing, thickly, mufflingly, each heavy flake as fat as a snowball. Everybody gasped at the cold but held each other close for warmth. Even Jennifer consented for Jake to hold her (for warmth).

"This is great. This is great!" Eddie exulted. He whisked across the crunching snow with Cally in his arms. "Shall we dance?"

The stars glittered like ice, so distant, so remote. And high above the students, the night was purest black. Lori gazed up and let the snowflakes dab her face, and she thought how small she was in the grand scheme of things, how tiny they all were. And it made her want to be someone, to do something, and the frosty air filled her lungs with strength.

"Hey, look!" Ben called out. "There's Grant!"

They could see the senior tutor's silhouette at his window, watching them.

"I'm going to remember him in my will," promised Eddie, "because if it wasn't for Grant, none of us would be here now."

"You're right," said Jake. "For once, Ed, you're right."

"But now that we are all here," said Ben, "and before we all die of pneumonia, I'd like to propose a toast."

"But we left our drinks in the rec room," protested Lori.

"Forget the drinks. Drinks don't matter. But what I'm about

to say *does* matter." Ben built the tension. "Just three little words."
He grinned and punched them out. "To Bond Team!"

"To Bond Team!" The others took up the cry, raised it to the
night, threw their arms around each other, and laughed and
clapped and cheered.

"Bond Team!" Ben yelled. "We're here to stay!"

But what the silent silhouette of their tutor thought of that,
no one could tell.

CHAOS IS COMING . . .

Turn the page for a sneak peek at

SPY HIGH:
MISSION TWO

CHAOS
RISING

Arriving Spring 2004 from
Little, Brown and Company

The room was screaming.

To be accurate, making noise was what Spy High's Intelligence Gathering Center did. The IGC was wired into every significant news network on the planet — as well as most of the insignificant ones — monitoring events across the globe as they happened, directly and immediately relaying the latest developments in human history to the school where Jonathan Deveraux and his team of tutors could decide what action, if any, the graduates of Spy High needed to take in order to protect and preserve the safety of mankind. Twenty-four hours a day, sometimes longer, the IGC echoed and reechoed with the sound of a million voices in a thousand languages. The members of Bond Team were used to that. They expected it.

But they didn't expect the horrors that greeted them today.

Terror and trauma on every continent. Carnage and calamity from North Pole to South. Apocalyptic images like nightmares come true were blazing from the screens around them. A hovertel tossed from the skies and hitting the earth like a fireball. Computer-controlled traffic colliding and exploding. The solar cities of the California coast plunging into darkness. And on every screen, the same soundtrack to disaster: the whole world screaming. For once, no translation was necessary. Death has a common language.

"What's happening?" Cally stared, shocked at the screens. "It looks like the end of the world."

Lori slipped her hand into Ben's. Even though he didn't think to squeeze it reassuringly, it still felt better there.

"Sir?" A dismayed Jake turned to Grant.

"Keep watching," the tutor instructed.

"I can't," Jennifer protested, unusually squeamish. "This is too . . . turn it off! Stop it now!"

The screens went dead. A second of silence, almost as disturbing as the screams. Then on every screen, multiplied and menacing, a man in a mask like a photographic negative, the reverse of a human face, and Bond Team knew why they were here.

"We have spoken," announced the man, "and our words have been heard in destruction, disorder, and death throughout the world. Our language is CHAOS, a language your laughable so-called governments will soon come to understand more clearly than ever before. CHAOS: The Crusade for Havoc, Anarchy, and the Overthrow of Society. We are the enemies of your petty and repressive systems of order, your laws, and your institutions." The man in the mask leaned closer. "Your days are numbered. Law and order will be no more. It is time for CHAOS. We have spoken, and you have heard. We will be silent now for a while, so that you may consider what has been said, but we will return with our demands. And do not think that you can stop us. We can attack anyone, anywhere, and at any time. CHAOS is coming. And there is nothing you can do."

"I don't know. We can shut this guy up for starters, can't we?" Eddie looked across the room. "Where's the 'off' switch?"

"It doesn't matter," Grant said, as the IGC went silent, on its own accord, for the second time. "That was the entire communication. A little over an hour ago, it interrupted every major television broadcast worldwide. It seems this organization is claiming responsibility for the sequence of disasters you've just witnessed. Worse, it seems to be promising more."

"Then they've got to be stopped," Ben said, rather obviously.

"We've already reassigned all graduate teams to this one case," Grant said, "and we're trying to trace the source of their signal, so far without success. Whatever masking program they're using, it must be state of the art or beyond. What we need, and quickly, is a lead."

"Which is where you come in, Bond Team." The video-screens were resurrected again. Now the grave, wise features of Jonathan Deveraux himself faced the six students, examining them steadily. "Your earlier encounter with a CHAOS agent may provide us with precisely the lead of which Senior Tutor Grant speaks."

Bond Team exchanged glances. As one, their minds drifted back to the past, to their last term. To their camping trip in the Wildscape. To their capture by Dr. Averill Frankenstein, the mad geneticist. And to their brief videoscreen dialogue with a similarly masked CHAOS agent.

It was rare for Deveraux to be seen by Spy High's students, and even when he was, it was only through a videoscreen. But for the founder to ask for help as explicitly as he was doing now was unprecedented. If they could only make a contribution toward the defeat of CHAOS, Ben thought, there'd need to be a special place in the Hall of Heroes set aside just for them, with himself, as team leader, tastefully prominent. But sadly, not even he dared to tell Deveraux anything but the discouraging truth: "I don't think there is anything, sir. We were fully debriefed after the event. . . ."

"I am aware of that, Stanton," said Deveraux. "I have the tapes."

"Of course, sir." Ben sounded embarrassed. "I only meant that I can't think of anything else."

"Were you not helpless in Frankenstein's gene chamber for

much of the time? Perhaps some of your teammates have more to contribute."

"Actually, sir," said Cally, feeling that Deveraux was being a little unfair, "I doubt we can add any more than Ben. The agent we saw said exactly the same kind of things as this one today. It could even be the same man, what with the mask and everything."

Deveraux uttered a disappointed sigh. With it, Ben's special place in the Hall of Heroes seemed to vanish. "Very well. But if anything does occur to you, to any of you, no matter how slight or inconsequential it might seem to be, bring it to the attention of Senior Tutor Grant at once. We must explore every possible outcome in this present crisis. We cannot rest until the threat of CHAOS is over."

Deveraux blinked out.

Stung by the founder's implicit criticism, Ben took charge. "Meeting," he hissed conspiratorially to the others. "The girls' room. In an hour. Before Weapons Instruction. Let's go through the Frankenstein business again, just in case." He was pleased to see the general nods of agreement. "Everyone be there, okay? *Everyone.*"

That was clear enough, Ben thought. *Time. Place. Purpose.* So it was a bit of a shock for him when Bond Team reconvened with one member short, and it was the last person he would have expected to be missing.

"Where's Lori?" he asked.

She sat in the rec room, but she could have been anywhere. Her eyes were open, but they weren't seeing her immediate environment.

Inside her head, Lori was back in Frankenstein's gene chamber.

She shuddered as she relived her ordeal. Pounding on unyielding glass. Trapped like a specimen in a jar. The gene gas itself, lapping at her ankles, rising to her knees, her thighs, a gray tide dragging at her helpless limbs. Tasting it, bitter and acrid in her mouth, when her lips had been pried open by the need to breathe. And worst of all, feeling it working on her, reshaping her, molding something new from the inside out, feeling herself drifting, her identity and her humanity drowning.

Lori squeezed her eyes shut, as if memories could be denied that way. Maybe some could, but not this one. The gene chamber was always going to be with her, a constant and chilling reminder of her own mortality.

She'd told Ben how she felt, of course. He'd been appropriately sympathetic — all concerned expressions, soothing hands, and calming kisses, but it was clear he hadn't really understood. And this from someone who'd been trapped alongside her in the gene chamber, who'd tasted the transforming gas with her. The experience hadn't seemed to have affected Ben, or if it had, he wasn't letting on. "But it's all right now, babe. It's all done with," he'd said. "We survived." Which was true. "The gene chamber's been destroyed." Also true. "You can forget about it now." Well, two out of three wasn't bad.

But she didn't want to go over it all again. Let the others meet up and discuss it if they wanted to. She'd make her excuses to Ben sometime later. For now, all she wanted to do was sit here quietly and not be disturbed.

Somebody else had other ideas.

"Vanessa? Vanessa, how charming of you to come."

To begin with, Lori didn't respond largely because her name was not Vanessa. But it was hard to remain oblivious when Gadge Newbolt plumped himself down in front of her, beaming as if he were meeting an old friend for the first time in years.

Gadge Newbolt, or Professor Henry Newbolt to be more accurate, had been the scientific genius behind virtually all of Spy High's technological marvels, hence his nickname: "Gadge" as in "gadget."

"Vanessa," he crooned again. Lori glanced behind her. No Vanessa here. "My dear."

Unfortunately, Newbolt's brilliant brain had burned out long ago, and his famous gray cells were heaped in his skull like ashes. Now he was little more than an old man in a white coat, allowed to wander the school's corridors at will as a kind of merciful reward for all he'd contributed in the past. Before he went senile.

Nowadays, though, Gadge tended only to talk to walls, not people. And he'd never before now, to Lori's knowledge, called anyone Vanessa.

"Professor Newbolt," she addressed him nervously, wondering where the "my dear" had come from. She'd been warned about old men in white coats.

"Professor . . . ? No, my dear," old Gadge laughed, "what happened to "Grandfather"? Call me Grandfather like you always used to."

Oops. Ben's meeting suddenly seemed quite important, after all. "Nice to see you, Professor, but I've got to be . . ." Lori stood, smiling falsely. And saw the hurt in the old man's eyes. His thin lips quivered.

"Don't go, Vanessa," he said. "Not so soon. Not again.

You've only just arrived, and you haven't been to see your old grandfather for such a long time."

"Professor, I'm not Vanessa." Lori's first thought was to set Gadge straight. But then his brow furrowed, and she realized it would probably cause less harm if she pretended and played along with his delusions.

"Vanessa?" A final plaintive plea.

"Yes, Grandfather?" she tried.

Gadge brightened again immediately, grasped her hands in his, and shook them as Lori resumed her seat. "Oh, it is good to see you, my dear. It's been too long. Your old grandfather was beginning to wonder whether you'd forgotten him."

May be some truth in there, Lori thought. She was determined to find out more about Gadge's past if she could. But for now: "Oh, no, I've been busy, that's all. Of course I'd never forget you."

"Vanessa, Vanessa." Gadge dabbed fat, wet tears from his eyes. "You always were a good girl. And I've been busy, too, very busy indeed. Come and see what your old grandfather has been doing. See what I've got to show you in my lab."

Now this was probably going too far. Gadge had hopped to his feet and was tugging eagerly at Lori's arm, and she knew she'd have to make an excuse now. Lessons resumed in a few minutes, and it wasn't a good idea to skip them. Miss a class at Spy High, and you could miss something that could save your life one day. She'd have to leave. But then Gadge let go of her anyway. His hands fluttered in the air like falling leaves.

"Vanessa?" he said pathetically. "Where is my lab? I can't seem to . . . where is it?" He was like a child parted from its parents in a vast and terrifying public place. "Vanessa, can you help me? Please help me. Take me to my lab."

Lori sighed. How could she refuse? She'd have to catch up on her Weapons Instruction later.

"It's all right," she said, taking the old man's hand. "Let's go to your lab, Grandfather."

"Grandfather?" If Ben's jaw dropped any lower, Lori would be able to inspect his tonsils from the other side of the room. "You actually called him *Grandfather*?"

"Well, yes, I didn't see why not, Ben, what else could I do?" She looked for support from Cally, who seemed eager to provide it by repeating her last words and nodding a lot — "That's right, what else could she do?" — and from Jennifer, who was sitting, glazed, on her bed and not registering any interest in the real world whatsoever.

"What else?" Ben wasn't convinced. "You could have suggested that the old man get some therapy and then joined us at Lacey Bannon's Weapons Instruction lesson, that's what else." Sometimes he just didn't understand Lori. Where was her sense of duty? If only everyone was more like himself.

"Oh, Ben," Lori sighed exasperatedly. "It wasn't as easy as that. You didn't see what poor Gadge was like. You weren't there."

"That's right," Cally echoed. "You weren't there."

"Sounds like Gadge wasn't all there, either," snorted Ben unsympathetically. "So what happened next? It doesn't take an hour to get from Gadge's lab to the weapons chambers. Take a diversion to help some old ladies across the street, Lori?"

"It's that caring attitude that makes me love you, Ben," she replied. "Actually, I couldn't get away at once. Gadge was so pleased that I was there. He wouldn't let me leave. He was like a little kid showing an adult his toys. Showed me all his latest inventions."

"I thought he wasn't supposed to have invented anything worthwhile for years."

"They were just boxes with wires poking out of them, some old batteries, circuits, and lights. Nothing. Junk. And yet, he believed they were something wonderful. He wanted me to admire them. So I did. It was all so sad, really."

"You're telling me. Humoring a senile old fool when you should have been with the rest of us learning something useful."

Lori laughed ironically. "What? How to kill people in interesting new ways?"

"Listen," Ben reprimanded, "when we're out on a mission, you're going to find a laser cannon a bit more of an asset than a cozy bedside manner. I doubt you're going to get too far with these CHAOS goons by calling them grandfather and smiling at them sweetly. Know what I mean?"

"Actually, I do know what you mean," Lori said, "which is why I left Gadge's lab as soon as I could. After a while, he became so absorbed in all his tinkering that he seemed to forget I was even there. Then as I was creeping out, he noticed me again, but he didn't call me Vanessa or anything. Didn't seem to recognize me at all. Just said this was a private lab and students weren't allowed. His mind had obviously wandered off again, so I did, too. Only by then, Weapons Instruction was already over. Dare I ask if I missed anything important?"

"I'm afraid you did," Ben said officiously. "Lacey introduced us to the latest version of the stasis rifle with infrared sights for shooting in the dark."

"Yeah? Well, I hope you'll be very happy together."

"Very funny," he grunted. Cally certainly seemed to think so. "Let's hope you find things just as amusing in the Gun Run next week. Stasis rifles are included, and this one counts for the Shield. Or maybe you think winning that is a joke as well now, Lori. And maybe I'll just leave you to it." How had his day come to this? It had started so well with the Wall, but since then, it had fallen apart. First Deveraux, now Lori. Frowning petulantly, Ben turned to go.

"Ben, I didn't —" Lori called after him.

The door slammed.

"Have you ever thought about trading him in for a more mature model?" Cally wondered aloud.

"I don't think I could." Lori blushed. "I don't think I'd want to. I know he can be difficult at times, and short with people, and intolerant, and a bit selfish . . ."

"Sorry, Lori," interrupted Cally, "but are you Ben's girlfriend or his analyst?"

"Only you should see him when we're alone." Lori blushed again, proudly. "Then you'd see a different Ben, a better Ben. He can be so gentle, so . . ."

"Yeah, well we don't want to go there, do we?" Cally laughed. "We'll take your word for it, won't we, Jen?"

"Anyway, I think I'd better . . ." Lori gestured after Ben. "I'd better apologize. Ben was right, really. I shouldn't have missed the lesson."

"What? No way." Cally shook her head in mock disbelief. "He stormed out. You go after him now, and we're talking personal humiliation. The way he spoke to you — let him come crawling back and apologize, Lori, assuming Ben Stanton's even physically capable of saying sorry. Let him know who's boss. That's what we'd do, isn't it, Jen?"

Cally and Lori both seemed to realize at the same time that Jennifer was not quite with them.

"Jennifer? Hello? Jen?"

IGC DATA FILE FBA 8320

"Men like Boromov Corbin and Pascal Z see technology as a means of reinforcing the divide between the rich and the poor, the haves and the have-nots of the world. They talk about technoimperialism, about the technologically advanced nations exploiting those countries that lack an industrial or scientific base. At the same time, this CHAOS organization seems to be going even further, disrupting technology as a way of destabilizing society itself. It seems clear to me that our entire way of life is facing a major crisis." Professor Talbot went on to say . . .

She didn't sleep the entire night. She didn't dare. To close her eyes would be to dream, and to dream, on this night more than any other night in the year, would be to invite the shadows in, to leave her defenseless before the tall, dark man — the man in the doorway.

So Jennifer lay on her back with her arms at her sides, as if she was practicing death, and stared at the ceiling as if it were the lid of a coffin.

And maybe she'd already surrendered. Maybe she'd fallen asleep without realizing it. With the room so black, it was difficult to tell for sure whether her eyes were open or closed. She thought she must be asleep because the doorway was suddenly before her with the man's shape in it. But perhaps she was still awake, and the man who chuckled like the rattle of a cobra was no longer content to remain in her dreams, in her past, but was emerging into the here and now to claim her. On this day of all days, that would be apt.

It was the anniversary of the day he'd claimed her parents.

Jennifer whimpered softly in her throat, twisted the sheets in her hands, and longed for daylight.

"You all right, Jen?" Jake asked at breakfast, trying to look behind her eyes to where the truth might lie. "I don't want to sound intrusive, but you look like you've seen a ghost."

"Could be worse," joked Ben. "Could have seen Eddie in the shower."

"Oh, very funny," Eddie huffed. "On the other hand, though, Jen, if you ever wanted to see me in the shower, I'm sure something could be arranged. You know, you could scrub my back . . ."

"You're better off scrubbing the whole idea," said Jake, a note of warning beneath the humor. "If you know what I mean."

"I'm fine, anyway," said Jennifer, not meeting anybody's eye. "Just let it go."

But Jake wasn't satisfied. If only Jennifer would allow him to get closer. He wanted to, she knew that, but still she kept shutting him out, as if there were a closed door between them that she didn't dare open. He decided to try again after martial arts, and if that didn't work, he'd keep on trying. Jake Daly didn't give up easily.

Today's lesson was kendo, the way of the sword. Not steel swords with killing blades, of course, but the *shinai*, the bamboo blade.

Bond Team prepared themselves. They donned the protective armor, adjusting and tightening the breastplates, tugging on the padded gloves, and hiding their faces behind the *men*, the face masks with steel grills.

Like bars, Jennifer found her blurred brain thinking as she fixed her *men* into place. Bars to imprison her, bars to suffocate her. She felt her breathing quicken, as though she'd been running a great distance and was about to collapse. But it wasn't just the grill that was confusing her, her sight was thick and muddy, too — nothing seemed clear around her. It was the lack of sleep, she realized, over many nights. She couldn't cope with it. And especially today, on the anniversary.

Mr. Korita, who like Bond Team was fully regaled in his *dogu* armor, drew them together and talked about the lesson. Jennifer wasn't following what he was saying. She glanced from side to side. Everybody looked the same, concealed with secret faces behind the bars. She couldn't tell who they were anymore. She couldn't even tell who she was.

Mr. Korita had said something. And then they were selecting their *shinai*. The sword felt good in her gloved hands, strong, true, something to rely on.

Her mind whispered a memory. *"Mom! Dad! Don't leave me!"*

And she suddenly realized the masked people surrounding her were laughing. And they were backing away from her, leaving her alone in the center of the gym with the little man who gave orders.

He was giving orders to her. His sword was raised in front of him. He wanted to fight her. She knew that she had to fight him and raised her own *shinai* accordingly. She wondered who he was.

Then he was at her, like lightning. Before she could even

move to defend herself, striking at both sides of her torso, the impact of each blow dulled by her armor but felt nonetheless. And then, with an expert and almost invisible twist of his *shinai*, he severed hers from her hand and sent it skittering across the floor.

Jennifer sensed the loss and scrambled after her sword.

The others were laughing at her. Or were they? Or was it just the thudding of blood in her ears? The pounding of fist on door. She groped for her weapon. On her knees, she clutched its handle and crouched.

Toward her approached a man in a mask, wielding a weapon.

And she knew who it was. She suddenly knew. It was him, the night man, the man in the doorway. He'd come for her at last. But he couldn't have her. He wouldn't take her. She was not weak, not like her parents. She'd made herself strong. She'd show him exactly how strong. She'd show them all.

A cry of rage and hurt and fury tore from her throat as Jennifer leapt to her feet. Her body shook with anger and hate.

Show him? She'd kill him.